If It Weren't
for Sebastian

If It Weren't for Sebastian

Jean Ure

DELACORTE PRESS/NEW YORK

Published by   *Allen County Public Library*
Delacorte Press   *Ft. Wayne, Indiana*
1 Dag Hammarskjold Plaza
New York, N.Y. 10017

This work was first published in Great Britain by The Bodley
Head, Ltd.

Library of Congress Cataloging in Publication Data
Ure, Jean.
If it weren't for Sebastion.
Summary: Maggie, the youngest daughter in a
family of doctors, longing to know more about life
outside the world of medicine, shocks her family with
her decision to break with tradition and take a
secretarial course.
[1. Emotional problems—Fiction] I. Title.
PZ7.U64If   1985   [Fic]
ISBN 0-385-29380-1
Library of Congress Catalog Card Number: 84-15568

Manufactured in the United States of America

First U.S.A. printing

1

2278075

"Honestly! Talk about rave—they practically went berserk. Anyone would think I'd said I wanted to go out and be a prostitute."

"Bad?" said Val.

"Bad?" said Maggie. "You should have heard them!"

"I suppose it was only to be expected."

"I didn't expect them to go mad."

Really, it had been quite incredible. One minute they had been having an ordinary, amicable family discussion, just the three of them, trying to work out how Pa could take on the new consultancy he'd been offered up in Birmingham without disrupting Maggie's final year at school down in the cushy southeast; the next, they'd gone crazy. Of course, she had known they wouldn't be pleased. When you had the misfortune to be saddled with a consultant anesthetist for a father and a mother who had once been a gynecologist, not to mention a married sister who was a GP, plus a brother who'd just qualified, plus another up at Leeds, doing things with test tubes, and you suddenly went and shattered the intellectual image by announcing that you were going to take a course in shorthand-typing—well, all right, perhaps it had come as a bit of a shock, but they didn't have to treat her as if she were a mental leper, for goodness' sake.

Val said: "Did you break it to them gently?"

"As gently as one can."

"Yes, but were you tactful? You know how elephantine you can be."

"Well, I didn't grovel on the floor if that's what you mean. On the other hand, I didn't yell it at them."

She had, in fact, said it quite coolly and casually, surprising even herself.

"Actually," she had said, "you don't need to bother about me. I've been meaning to tell you for a day or two now . . . I've changed my mind about the university, so the extra year won't be necessary."

There had been a silence, while they both turned their heads, very slowly and deliberately, to look at her.

"What I mean is . . . I don't see why I couldn't go into an apartment or something. Down here, I mean. I wouldn't want to come and live in Birmingham."

They had ignored that bit. In a high, sharp, knotted sort of voice, which ought to have been immediately recognizable as a danger signal, Ma had said: "What do you mean, you've changed your mind?"

Pa, marginally quicker on the uptake and never one for wasting breath on futilities, had contented himself with a curt "Rubbish! It's already been decided. . . . Now, look, is there any reason why she shouldn't go to Dot's and come in to school by train every day? She could—"

"Yes," Maggie had said. "I told you: I've changed my mind. Anyway, who decided? *I* certainly didn't."

She had never decided. She had just gone along with the idea because it seemed to be expected—because it was what all the rest of the family had done.

"It wasn't me that made the decision," said Maggie. "It was you."

"So may one inquire," had said Pa, all cold and full of sarcasm, "what one has decided upon instead?"

This was the part which really needed careful handling.

"I'd thought of enrolling at the Tech."

Ominous quiet. Then Pa, very stony: "To do what precisely?"

"Well . . . I thought perhaps . . . a commercial course?"

"What kind of"—perceptible pause before he could bring himself to repeat the words—"commercial course?"

Even then it was in quotes, as if it were something nasty. Ma, trying hard (or simply not willing to credit it), had said brightly: "Business studies? Management? That sort of thing?"

"No, I—I hadn't quite thought of that."

"What then?"

Here goes. Either one said it or one didn't. There wasn't any point in wrapping it up in fancy language.

"Shorthand-typing actually."

"Shorthand-*typing?*"

That was when the storm had really broken. A daughter of *ours?* Doing shorthand-*typing?*

"You must be mad! You'll be bored to death within a week."

"Why should I be?"

"Just a glorified piece of office equipment."

"Not necessarily. A job's what you make it."

"Huh!"

"Well, it is. It doesn't *have* to be boring."

"Typing other people's semiliterate letters?"

"If they were, I'd make them literate."

"And that's what you've spent the last twelve years at school for? To play wet nurse to some half-witted businessman?"

"I'm not such a great intellect as all that."

"But, Maggie, you've got three A-levels! You can't be a shorthand-typist with three A-levels!"

"I don't imagine for one moment that I *have* got three A-levels."

"Of course you have! Miss Stanhope said you'd get them standing on your head. That's been the whole trouble. All along. Too easy. You and Chris, the pair of you— if you'd had to slog, like Dot and Jesse—it meant something to them. They had to work for it. You! You just sail through everything. You take it for granted. There isn't any effort. Well, let me tell you, my girl—"

On, and on, and on.

"Lunacy! Sheer lunacy!"

"Something vocational, I could understand—"

"But *this?*"

"And why? She hasn't even told us why!"

Telling them why had been almost as difficult as telling them what. She couldn't say she wanted to get out and earn money. One simply didn't do things "just for the money." Not in their family. Very frowned upon. And anyway, it wouldn't have been true, any more than it would have been true to say she was sick of school or sick of studying, because she wasn't. School at times could admittedly be a bit of a drag, but the senior year was pretty much of a law unto itself, and she was almost certain to have been made joint head with one of the boys—Stuart Gibbs, in all probability—and even though

Chris would have hooted, it would have been something, in secret, to be proud of. And Stuart Gibbs wasn't really too bad. She wouldn't actually have minded.

So why? Her own brand of rebellion? She had toyed for a moment with the idea of claiming it was so—they would have latched on to it eagerly, would have analyzed it, dissected it, talked it out from every angle—but not even rebellion was the real answer. Rebellion was only part of it. A way of rationalizing.

The real reason was something far more difficult to put into words. It had something to do with . . . living. But *really* living. Finding out what it was all about. Men, relationships. That sort of thing. Val knew about it. Val had known for years. Not Maggie. Maggie with the astronomical IQ and the ten exams at ordinary level and the three (probable) at advanced—*she* didn't know. She didn't know anything at all except how to pass exams. And what use was that to anyone? Really, when it came down to it? What *use* was it? She was nearly eighteen, for heaven's sake, and she'd never even had a boyfriend. Not a proper boyfriend. Not like Val. It was time she got out into the world and did a bit of discovering.

She and Val had talked it over. Val had said: "I mean, if you're absolutely dead *set* on doing medicine—"

But she wasn't. She never had been.

"It was them." *They* were the ones who were set on it; they were the ones who took things for granted. She would probably have been far happier doing general arts, along with Val.

"And let's face it, you'd be middle-aged before you were through . . . you don't want to end up like Dot."

No, let Dot be a solemn warning: settled for life in Chislehurst, before she was even thirty. What had she ever seen? Ever done? Other than marry Francis and get herself pregnant? Some sort of experience *that* was.

"At least with secretarial," said Val, "you can get it over with. Even at the Tech it only takes a year. And once you're qualified, you can go virtually anywhere."

Yes, that was the argument: You could go *any*where. She had tried it out on the parents. It had met with loud, scoffing noises.

"Anywhere!"

"Doing what?"

"Making the tea?"

"Bashing a typewriter?"

"Being a *door*mat?"

"For heaven's sake, girl!"

"As if you can't go anywhere when you're a doctor."

"Only get through your finals and you can go any-where at all."

"Yes," she had said, "but I want to go *now*. While I'm still *young*. I want to go to America. Val and I—"

That had been a blunder. Her mother had said: "Val! I might have known it! I've said from the beginning that that relationship would do you no good. Why on earth you ever had to get yourself tied up with that girl in the first place—vain, silly, shallow, not a brain in her head. Why couldn't you have found someone more your equal? She's done nothing but drag you down. Just be-cause *she* can't get through her A-levels—"

Maggie had seen red at that. Her temper was as explo-sive as her mother's, and she wasn't having Val maligned. She and Val had been friends since their very first term at Tennyson's, since their very first morning, when the roll had been called and they had been Margaret Easter and Valerie Flowers, and Easter Flowers forevermore. But it wasn't only being Easter Flowers. It was six years of growing up together—six years of confidences and discoveries, of shared experience.

She had always known her mother didn't think much of Val. Her mother never did think much of anybody who was pretty and cared how she looked. She would have liked Maggie to make friends with someone like Olga Franks, who wore thick-lens spectacles and braces and chewed her fingernails to the quick and was the most monumental fright ever to have walked the face of the earth. But that didn't matter, because she was brilliant. Val was beautiful and slender, with sea-green eyes and red-gold hair. She did tend to get a bit lost when it came to the realms of higher mathematics, but she certainly wasn't dumb, and it wasn't fair to say she'd dragged Maggie down. How could she have done that if the Stanhope said she could get three A-levels standing on her head? How could she do that if Val had dragged her down? Or did they think, perhaps, that without Val she could have bagged a round half dozen? For crying out *loud*.

"And anyway, what do you know about Val's A-levels? She could have passed, and I could have failed, and then you'd laugh the other side of your face."

"Oh"—her mother, at her most annoying, as she frequently could be, had given one of her tinkling trills, pitched high with pretended amusement—"I hardly count *handi*crafts and *hair*dressing."

"She's not taking handicrafts and hairdressing! Why are you always such an intellectual *snob?*"

"I like people to have brains. I see nothing wrong in that. What I cannot stand is the sort of bird-witted conceit which all too often betokens the total lack of them."

Maggie had felt the palms of her hands begin to grow sticky with suppressed rage. She knew that one couldn't fly at one's own mother and throttle her, but the temptation was very great.

"Girls like you don't deserve education if at the end of the day you're just going to throw it all overboard. Much good it does us, fighting for equal rights. When I was at school, a female could still count herself lucky to get any form of higher education at all. I had to *plead* with my parents to let me go on and become a doctor."

"Yes, and where's it got you? Dishing out free pills two mornings a week at the family planning? Big deal!"

Pa, who as a rule steered very well clear of female squabbles, had banged upon the table at this and shouted: "That's enough, that's enough! How dare you speak to your mother like that? She's sacrificed a career bringing you people up."

"So what am I supposed to do? Cut off my arm or something? *I* didn't ask it of her."

"Then all the more reason for showing a little gratitude."

"All right! Gratitude, gratitude! I'm exceedingly blessed to have a mother who has made such a sacrifice . . . but I still don't reckon it does much for equal rights, so what's she going on at *me* for?"

From that point on it had all become rather squalid. Left to themselves, Maggie and her mother quite often quarreled, but in general, as a family, the Easters were civilized. They believed in keeping one's cool and having reasoned discussion rather than simply bawling. The last occasion on which Maggie could remember a row quite so violent, quite so undisciplined, had been years and years ago, when Chris had been caught cheating on a

Latin exam. Even then it hadn't been the cheating so much as what they called the *need* to cheat. That had been the real crime. Just as today the real crime was not Maggie's yelling things at her mother, but Maggie's "denying her intellectual capacity."

"Denying my intellectual capacity! Ye gods!" She rolled her eyes heavenward. "Did you ever hear such pseud talk?"

"Eggheads," said Val.

"Boneheads, more like. Can't see anyone's point of view but their own."

"Well, I suppose it has to be admitted that you are quite reasonably cleverish."

"Not compared with Olga Franks."

"Oh, well! That freak."

Tolerant for once, Maggie said: "She can't help it."

"She can help it. Nobody *has* to go around like that. Great greasy wads of hair and spots all over her face."

"It's all right for you," said Maggie. "You never get them."

"Only because I don't stuff myself with chocolates. You wouldn't if you didn't, but you will insist. *And* you wouldn't have fat thighs."

Maggie pulled a face. Fat thighs were her bane. Miss Holder, in gym, had looked at them and said: "Nonsense! Perfectly normal!" but she knew that they weren't. Val's thighs were hardly any bigger at the top ends than they were down at the knees.

"Soon as we start college, I'll go on a diet. Honest. I promise. You can hold me to it."

"Ha-ha," said Val. "I've heard that one before. Anyway, don't talk too soon. Just wait till Stanhope's had a go at you . . . you'll be back all meek and mild, running the school with old goody-goody Gibbs."

"Not me," said Maggie.

She had weathered the row with her parents: it would take more than Miss Stanhope to break her. It had been her father who had finally brought the disgusting scene to a close by announcing that he couldn't be bothered to argue with her anymore.

"Go your own way, do your own thing. You'll learn sooner or later."

Her mother, tartly, had said: "Yes! And suppose it happens to be later rather than sooner?"

"That's her lookout. I'm not going to force her."

She was grateful, at any rate, for that, but she did rather resent the patronizing assumption that in the end she would come around to their way of thinking. It was exactly what they always assumed: *We know best,* so that even while they were letting you go your own way and do your own thing, they were sitting up there, lofty on Olympus, serenely awaiting the moment when you discovered your mistake. Well, this time there wasn't going to be any mistake. She had made up her mind, and nobody and nothing were going to talk her into changing it.

2

Nobody did talk Maggie into changing her mind, though it was hardly for want of trying. Chris, home for the summer vacation, said: "Haven't you ever heard of the microchip? You'll find yourself redundant before you've even started. Computers are the thing. Make a packet in computers."

"I don't want to make a packet. I'm not interested in making packets. I just want to be me."

"You could still be you and make a packet."

"No, I couldn't."

"Yes, you could."

"Well, I don't want to."

"You don't want to make money?"

"No! That is—not particularly. No."

Chris scratched his ear. "Strange, unambitious lady," he said.

"Yes, well, that's me. I'm obviously the black sheep. You've got to have *one* black sheep; every family with pretensions always does."

Two days later Dot rang up from Chislehurst in one of her mumsy flusters.

"Maggie, darling, I've just heard the news." (News!

Did it really rate the headlines? TRAGEDY HITS DOCTOR'S FAMILY: YOUNGEST DAUGHTER LETS THE SIDE DOWN.) "Mags, are you quite *sure* you know what you're doing? I don't want to preach and sound big-sisterly, but it is your whole future."

Quite, thought Maggie. *It is* my *whole future: mine.* One forgave Dot because she couldn't help it. Well-meant interference in other people's affairs came as naturally to her as sleeping and breathing (one only hoped that after she'd had the baby, she would have other matters to occupy her), but all the same there were times when one did wish that she wouldn't.

"Honestly, Mag, I can't help feeling you're making a terrible mistake. Shorthand-typing really isn't you."

Why wasn't it? What did Dot know about it?

Aggressively she said: "Why not?"

"Well, you know it isn't. You're not a sitting-at-a-desk type. You're an up-and-doing type. You always have been. Ever since you were a little girl. Especially with people. Look at all your lame ducks. Look at old Mrs. Thing, the way you used to go and sit with her, and that awful man that smelled that you brought home that time and wanted us to feed. . . . Look at that dreadful fat child at primary school—the one you insisted come on holiday with us."

"Melanie Onslow. I used to bully her."

"You didn't bully her! You took pity on her. You're always taking pity on people. Look at Val."

The bristles went up immediately. What did she mean, look at Val? She hadn't taken pity on Val. Val wasn't a lame duck. Very far from it. She might have been just at first, perhaps, way back in the mists, on account of only having been to some tin-pot little private school with a dozen pupils and not knowing anything about netball or hockey or how to parse a sentence, but Val had blossomed over the years. It was no longer busy, bustling Maggie, popular in spite of her bossiness, and dim, dreary Val, despised as a nobody. Now they were equals. Maggie was still busy and bustling, and on the whole people liked her, but since Val had come into her own, as an acknowledged beauty and expert in matters of fashion, she had had to stop being quite so bossy. If anything, these days, it was Val who bossed her. "You simply cannot be seen in that *ghastly* coat" and *"Really,* Maggie, your *hair*—"

"Surely you remember," said Dot coaxingly, "how you used to play at hospitals? You always used to make all your little friends be the patients because you had to be the doctor."

All her little friends! For crying out *loud.*

"That was when I was about two years old, and anyway, it was conditioning." If the parents had been coal miners, she would have played at coal mining—and all the little friends would have had to be pit ponies. Or the coal face. "It's a very funny thing," she said, trying not to sound irritable because it *was* only Dot and she really couldn't help it, "the way everyone around here seems to think they know me better than I do."

Next day—by, of course, the purest chance—Jesse turned up unexpectedly from London, saying he wasn't on duty until 9:00 A.M. the following day and had felt like a spot of home cooking to "put the stuffing back into me." Pa said: "Slave labor, eh?"

"You can say that again! Haven't stopped for the last forty-eight hours."

Ma said: "But it is worth it, isn't it? It is *satisfying?"*

Ma was always so obvious.

After supper, casually, Jesse turned to Maggie and said: "Feel like a stroll? Take Bess around the block?" Her heart sank. Not Jesse as well. He was her very favorite of all her family. Like Dot, he was gentle, patient, and persevering (unlike Chris and Maggie, who could be ill-tempered and were frequently slapdash), but Jesse had the blessed gift of knowing when not to obtrude. Or so she had always thought. Don't say that even he, now, was going to start nagging.

No, Jesse never nagged. He didn't even mention it until they were three-quarters of the way around the block and Bess held up the proceedings by sitting down in the middle of the footpath to investigate herself. Even then he didn't censure or preach. He said: "Ma wants me to have a go at you."

"Don't tell me," said Maggie.

"Don't intend to."

She felt a surge of relief. "Not going to lecture me?"

"Would there be any point?"

She grinned. "Not really."

"Then I shan't bother."

"But I suppose you still think I'm beyond the pale?"

"Oh, I wouldn't say that. Not beyond the pale exactly. Naturally I shan't be able to introduce you to any of my friends or acknowledge you in company, but I don't believe there should be any actual necessity for cutting you dead."

Beneath the banter she knew that Jesse, just as much as the rest of them, had doubts about what she was doing. He wouldn't set himself up in judgment, but even he thought she was wasting her talents. She accused him of

it, bitterly. "You think I'm doing something that's beneath me."

"Does it matter what I think?"

"Yes!" Of course, it mattered. What Jesse thought mattered to her almost more than anything.

"But not enough to make you change your mind?"

She frowned and was silent. Jesse hunched a shoulder.
"So it's your decision. Your life. The main thing is that
you should be happy."

Bess raised her head from where it had been buried,
sat for a moment clattering her teeth in pensive fashion,
finally heaved herself up, and indicated her willingness
to go on.

"If you'd just promise me one thing," said Jesse. "If
you *don't* find it makes you happy, don't be too proud to
say so. No one's going to sneer or jeer."

No? But they wouldn't half have a field day with the
"I told you so's."

"There's no disgrace attached to admitting you've
made a mistake."

"I'm not *making* a mistake," said Maggie.

Her A-levels came through, and she'd got all three. In
tones of gloomy satisfaction her mother said: "There.
They probably won't accept you for a shorthand course
with three A-levels. They'll say you're above it."

"People with degrees," said Maggie, "do shorthand
courses."

"Only as a means. Not as an end."

"This is only as a means. So that I can travel."

"Of course, *doctors* never travel. *Doctors* never go to
America. . . . Wait till you've spoken to Miss Stanhope.
She'll tell you what a fool you're being."

Miss Stanhope did tell her, and at some length, but having told her and been met with what she chose subsequently to describe as "bovine intransigence," she followed in the steps of Maggie's father and dismissed her as not worth bothering with.

"I'm afraid I can't waste my time trying to convince girls who don't wish to be convinced. I have far more deserving cases making demands upon me. Girls who are really interested in extending themselves. Achieving something. . . . Go and do your shorthand-typewriting. You will be frustrated beyond measure, but you will have only yourself to blame. I need hardly say how grievously you disappoint me."

"So that's it," said Maggie.

"You mean you really told the old bat where to go?"

"Well"—honesty compelled her to admit it—"it more or less ended up with her telling me . . . practically a case of 'Never darken these doors again.' "

"Some hardship," said Val.

"Oh, I'm absolutely heartbroken. Shan't be able to take part in the old girls' sack race—"

"Or flash yourself around at Open Day—"

"Or roam the corridors in search of nostalgia—"

"Or have your name written up as head girl."

"Almost more than I can bear! Don't keep on, you'll have me in tears."

"You would have been head girl," said Val.

"Then I've been saved from a fate worse than death, haven't I?"

"I don't know." Val sounded suddenly dubious. "It wouldn't have suited *me,* but you are still awfully school-oriented."

"I'm not!" That was the direst insult ever. "I don't care two cents about the blasted place."

"I just hope that you're sure."

"Of course I'm sure!"

Hadn't they mapped it all out? One year at college, one year of temping, just to get their hands in, then off and away wherever the fancy took them?

"You don't have to worry about me," said Maggie. "I know where *I'm* going."

She thought she did—but that was before she met Sebastian.

3

At the beginning of August the parents moved up to Birmingham. They left the house in the hands of real estate agents, Chris staying with friends, and Maggie parked on Dot—but only, heaven be praised, for a limited period. She had managed to talk them around on the question of lodgings.

"Going by train would take forever—it's a two-mile slog before you even reach the station. Anyway, they won't want me cluttering the place up once they've got the baby."

Dot had said: "Oh, Maggie, really! You wouldn't clutter, you'd be a positive help."

She didn't want to be a positive help; she wanted to live by herself in her own place and be independent.

"I should *feel* that I was cluttering," she said. "And it's still a two-mile slog."

The parents, at any rate, had not taken much persuading. They had never been ones to fuss or cluck, one had to grant them that much. Self-reliance ran brains and intellect a close second in their scale of values (which was why, for almost three years, Maggie had been an enthusiastic member of the Robin Patrol, learning round-

turns-and-two-half-hitches and how to rub sticks together to produce fire, until Val at last had convinced her
of the childish futility of such things and borne her off to
the local disco instead).

It was Dot, rather than the parents, who went all
mother-hennish, but with Dot it was only to be expected. The parents, bound up in their own arrangements, said she could do whatever she liked (the implica-
tion being that they had washed their hands of her?) so
long as she didn't take drugs, especially not heroin, and
Pa drove her into the hospital with him one morning to
make her look upon some addicts and be forewarned.
After that, they evidently considered her fully equipped
to deal with life, for they went off without so much as a
backward glance, only telling Dot to "make sure that
she's settled" and Maggie to "let us know if and when
you come to your senses. It might not be too late even
now." She didn't ask too late for what? They had done
that scene; she didn't want a repetition.

The Technical College helped with accommodations,
providing lists of addresses which students could consult
before the term began. Mostly they were for apartments
or for "two sharing."

"Only wish we could," said Val when Maggie put the
idea to her.

"Don't you think they'd let you?"

"Doubt it. Fork out for rooms when they keep me at
home for free?"

"You could always try asking them." Val's parents
weren't short of a penny or two. They had bought her a
real fur coat for her birthday and promised her her own
car next year. As an only child she could usually get
what she wanted. Perhaps on this occasion she didn't

really want; Maggie had the suspicion that if she had asked at all, she hadn't asked very hard. But Val always had been one for her creature comforts. Difficult to imagine her slumming it.

For a while it looked as though Maggie's cherished independence was going to turn into a room at the YWCA (much favored by Dot: "At least I'd know that you were safe"), but then at the eleventh hour she was granted a reprieve. In an old house in Station Road— naturally at the wrong end, right up at the very top of the hill, overlooking the gasworks and the marsh and almost underneath the railway bridge, but who cared about that?—she came upon a vacant room. According to the Spanish caretaker, who lived on the premises, the only reason it was vacant was that the boy who had been going to have it had been involved in a motorcycle crash and wasn't expected out of the hospital for at least another two months. She tried her best to feel decently sorry for him, but it was difficult when he was so totally unknown and she so desperate. He had probably been going too fast anyway. Pa said motorcycles were the menace of the age.

The room was perfect, almost exactly how she'd envisaged it. It had a gas fire, with a meter that took coins; a small electric stove, with hot plate and grill (and another meter); a washbasin, discreetly hidden behind a pink plastic curtain; a table, a chair, a sofa bed (linen all supplied); a cupboard for food, another for clothes; a shelf for books; and double floor-length windows, which opened onto a small balcony.

Across the road, directly opposite, she could see the start of the long row of shops that went straggling back down the hill to the center of town. Newsstand, super-

market, launderette, something that looked as if it might
be fish and chips. She pictured herself using them, calling
in at the newsstand for a paper every morning on her
way to college, stopping off at the supermarket every
evening, taking her clothes to the launderette—Dot had
said she must bring her washing back to Chislehurst every weekend, but Dot would have enough to do with
babies' diapers, and in any case she hadn't the least intention of running back and forth to Chislehurst. She
hoped there would be more exciting ways of passing the
time.

As she turned back into the room—*her* room—Val,
whom she had brought with her, caught her eye and
grimaced, nodding her head as she did so in the direction
of one of the walls. Expecting damp patches or mildew at
the very least, Maggie followed her gaze. The Spanish
caretaker stood watchful in the doorway.

"Lovely wallpaper," said Val.

Maggie felt a faint twinge of irritation. Did she have
to? Straw-colored baskets of sickly green fruit on a pink
background might not be everyone's choice, but so
what? What did a bit of wallpaper matter? It was the
room itself which was important. Anyway, she could always put up her bullfight posters and her full-length
chart of the human skeleton; they would cover it up soon
enough.

She said that she would take the room and wrote out
her very first check, for two weeks' rent, from her new
checkbook. Pa had said to let him know how much it
was, and he would transfer sufficient funds to cover it for
the term. She felt good having her own bank account,
even if it was only an extension of pocket money; she
felt even better having her own room. She would have

screamed before long if she'd had to go on living with
Dot and Francis. Francis was nice but fortyish and fusty
—did nothing but read medical journals and champ on
his pipe—and Dot had recently developed a maddening
habit of chasing after people with dustpan and brush,
sweeping up. One thing about Ma, she had never been
house-proud. With four children and a big, hairy dog,
she had always said it wasn't worth it.

They went back downstairs with the housekeeper and
stood waiting while she disappeared through a door at
the end of the passage in search of spare keys and a rent
book.

"Wonder what the rest of the house is like," said Val.
"Students?"

"Could be middle-aged spinsters, spying on you all
the time to make sure you don't have Men."

Again she felt that faint twinge of irritation.

"Yes, and it could be full of sex maniacs in dirty rain-
coats . . . might just as well look on the bright side."

As they went down the front steps, Maggie impor-
tantly jangling her new set of keys, they paused to study
the names of the various occupants, as indicated by the
battery of bells, each with its individual card stuck in a
frame.

Basement: Fuentes

"Must be the housekeeper."

Ground Floor: Nkala/Mbengwai

"Students," said Maggie.

First Floor:

"That's me."

Second Floor: Mr. & Mrs. Grace

"Married couple." Val dismissed them. "Boring."

Mezzanine:

"What's mezzanine?"

"Not sure. Something in between?"

Sebastian Sutton

"Wonder what he does?"

"Oh, he'll be your sex maniac. . . . Hey! How about these?" Val jabbed a finger at "Third Floor," where the piece of card, cavalierly printed in green felt tip pen, read: "Mick Waters & Paula Rose." "That looks more promising," said Val. "Better not let poor old Dot get an eyeful. She'll fall into a panic, thinking it's a house of ill repute."

Dot, fortunately, when she "settled Maggie in" the following Sunday, the day before she was due to start at college, was far too busy checking things—checking the sheets, checking the fire, checking the bathroom—to pay any attention to names written by the sides of bells. The only people to cross their path were a young man in a dark suit, and a girl dressed soberly all in brown, like a Plymouth Brother Maggie had once known who said that brightness in dress was a sin. The young man inclined his head, very polite and formal, and the girl smiled, but rather tightly, as if it hurt her lips to stretch them. Maggie wondered if she, too, were a Plymouth Brother—and then promptly unwondered it again. Hadn't she made a new rule for herself only last term? *I will not be prejudiced?* She did hope, though, that they weren't Mick Waters and Paula Rose. It would be too disappointing. Dot, in her Dottish way, said: "Well! They looked like a pleasant young couple. I was scared they might all turn out to be long-haired weirdos." With any luck, thought Maggie, some of them just might.

"Now, you will ring me, won't you?" said Dot.

"Yes, yes! I'll ring." Anything to keep her happy.

"And make sure you always lock your door at night—don't let anyone in unless you know who it is."

"No, Dot."

"And keep a special purse for the meters; otherwise, you'll find yourself running out."

"Yes, Dot."

"And whatever you do, don't forget to eat."

Forget to eat! Val might say it would be better if she did, but for all her great intellect Maggie was practical. She wasn't one for daydreaming while the milk boiled over and the toast went up in flames. No danger of her starving herself.

"And, Maggie"—heavens! more?—"not playing Holy Joe, but you will be careful, won't you?"

Now what did she mean by that?

She knew what she meant by that.

In short, *Beware of men.*

For crying out loud! Did this sister of hers really believe she didn't know how to take care of herself? After all those gruesome, clinical, textbook lectures? With a mother who dished out free pills two mornings a week at the family planning?

"It's awfully easy," said Dot, "to get carried away. Especially when you're on your own for the first time."

Maggie wondered if Dot had been carried away by Francis. Somehow it was not easy to imagine. Poor old Dot! She grinned, reassuringly.

"If all the men in the place," she said, "are like the one we just saw, then I don't think you've anything much to be worried about."

4

Starting as she meant to go on, Maggie was out of bed the following morning almost before the alarm clock had finished its alarming. Her clothes lay ready over the back of the chair—new scarlet sweater, knitted specially for her by Dot (Dot's knitting being pretty good) and her own favorite pair of jeans, which were big and baggy and did wonders for fat thighs. She thought of all the Tennysonians, climbing into their bottle green, and for a second she had a pang, picturing them all marching into the hall, wondering who would have been made head girl instead of her, but only for a second. Life at the moment was too full for regrets.

Indeed, she hadn't realized quite how much there would be to do in the mornings. Not only wash face, clean teeth, brush hair, but fill kettle, make coffee, get breakfast—*breakfast.* Yes. Bit of a moral problem there. Torn between her promise to Dot and her promise to Val —between a desire, on the one hand, to gorge herself on buttered toast, and an equal desire, on the other, to be slim as a willow wand and the envy of all—she compromised in the end and ate half an unsweetened grapefruit and a couple of crackers. By ten o'clock her stomach would be rumbling, but at least the inches would be coming off.

On her way down the road she called in rather self-consciously at the newsstand and bought a copy of *The Guardian,* for no better reason than that Pa wouldn't have it in the house. He said: "Give me *The Times* or give me the *Mirror,* but none of this wishy-washy muck in between." That was the trouble with Pa. Intolerant.

At the gates of the Technical College she met Val, trim and elegant in pleated skirt and a velvet jacket. Suddenly she had doubts about the wisdom of jeans. Val plainly also had doubts. She didn't say anything, but Maggie knew her well enough to sense disapproval. Her heart sank when they entered the spinach-tiled classroom that was to be theirs for the duration of the course and found about twenty other girls all demurely bedressed and beskirted. Not a jean in sight. She had obviously dropped yet another of her famous sartorial bricks. Val had told her once that "it's not so much that you lack dress sense as a sense of which dress for which occasion." It seemed that she was right. Now she would have everyone looking at her and thinking she had set out on purpose to be different.

"It is meant to be a *secretarial* course," whispered Val. "You wouldn't turn up for an interview wearing jeans, would you?"

Glumly she thought that she probably would. If anyone could put a foot in it, it was she.

Among all the twenty-odd girls in the course no fewer than four were also from Tennyson's. They didn't seem especially surprised to see Val but exclaimed with embarrassing loudness at the sight of Maggie.

"What are you doing here?"

"Thought you were one of Stanhope's pets?"

"Thought you were one of the brainy ones?"

"Never tell me you failed A-levels!"

It was Val who set them right. "Of course she didn't. She got all three."

Maggie cringed. She could understand that Val, not caring about A-levels for herself, was prepared to take a proprietary pride in Maggie's, just as Maggie, not caring about prettiness (or at least, not enough to make her jealous), could be proud of the fact that Val was a beauty; nonetheless, she would rather not have had to start off with the label "brainy" attached to her. She wished, now, that she hadn't bought that *Guardian.* No one else had any sort of newspaper at all.

For about ten minutes they stood around in protective groups—a cluster from Heathfield, three from the High, the six from Tennyson's. Then the door opened, and a teddy bear-shaped man appeared in a thick, hairy suit and introduced himself as Mr. Parker, the principal of the Commerce Department. He said: "Sit down, young ladies. Find yourselves seats." Maggie thought, how odd to be called young ladies. At school it had mostly been "you lot" or "people." She wasn't too sure about "young ladies." It sounded prissy.

Val tugged at her sleeve and said: "Sit!" Meekly she sat. Val, being Val, had bagged the best couple of desks, over by the window at the back.

The teddy bear man embarked on an introductory speech, telling them about the college, about the course, about the exams they would be expected to take and the sorts of jobs they could look forward to getting. At the end of the year, he said, before they were let loose upon the world, they all would have to take a turn in something called the practice office, where he would give them dictation and they would learn how to make telephone calls and use all the office equipment. For some ghastly reason, while everyone else was sitting there, absorbed in the thought of making telephone calls, Maggie had the insane urge to start giggling. It was only Val digging her in the ribs and hissing, "What's the matter?" that brought her to her senses.

After Mr. Parker, a brisk middle-aged lady, whom he introduced as Miss Everton, the course supervisor, came to give them schedules and sell books. She also took the roll as if they were back at school, the only difference being that now everyone was "miss." *Miss* Easter, *Miss* Flowers. (It had the usual reaction.) Miss Everton said that when they answered the telephone, they must always be sure to announce themselves as "Miss So-and-So," never just Christian names. Maggie found that troubling because both the parents had been very firm about *not* announcing oneself as Miss So-and-So. Pa had caught her at it one day, when she was much younger than she was now, and had nearly hit the roof. He had drummed it into her then: "You can say 'Dr. Easter's daughter,' or you can say 'Margaret Easter,' but never, *never* let me hear you say 'miss.' "

She ventured to query the point with Miss Everton (everyone turned to stare), who said that it was "up to your boss. If he likes to call you by your Christian name, then by all means announce yourself as Margaret Easter. If he doesn't, then best just stick to plain 'miss.' There is a growing tendency these days toward informality, but I don't personally care for it." Maggie wondered why not.

(She also wondered why the word "boss" made her hackles rise. *I shall never call anyone boss,* she thought.)

The schedules were also reminiscent of school except that the subjects had a strange, unschoollike ring. Their schedule for that first Monday was:

> Commerce
> Shorthand
>
> Break
>
> Accounts
> Shorthand
> Typing
>
> Break for lunch
>
> Typing
> English
> Office practice

Since they had already used up the first two periods in talking, they started straight in on the third, which was called accounts and was taken by Mr. Parker in his hairy suit. After A-level maths, accounts seemed a bit like going back to juniors. Mr. Parker kept saying, "Well, Miss Easter, I'm sure *you* can give us the answer." It made everyone, in all probability, want to grind her teeth, and Maggie herself crawl under the desk.

Shorthand, however, quickly redressed the balance. Miss Everton took one look at the mess of hieroglyphics which Maggie had copied off the board into her new shorthand notebook—upward strokes and downward strokes, heavy ones and light—and said: "Really, Miss Easter, you'll have to do better than *that.* Look at Miss Flowers's. See how neat it is." Val's *was* neat. All the strokes were the same length, all leaning at the same angle. She looked at her own, and it was quite horrible.

But then Val had always been good at art; Maggie couldn't draw a pig in a poke.

"I can see you're not a natural," said Miss Everton.

She wasn't a natural at typing either. Her fingers plonking on the keys were like big, insensitive sausages. You needed fingers like Val's, slender and supple, so that they could move quickly. Miss Everton said: "Practice will make perfect." Maggie reminded herself that it was but a means to an end.

At lunchtime, in the cafeteria, where Val made her eat a ham salad and plain yogurt, they met up with students from other faculties. The rest of their year mostly sat together; Val and Maggie chose a table apart. Val was never one for going with the crowd, and Maggie was not averse to keeping her distance from the other Tennysonians, at least until such time as they had grown accustomed to her being there and could gaze upon her without cries of wonderment.

While they were eating, a young man asked if he might join them and promptly sat down opposite Val. Young men generally did sit down opposite Val. This particular young man was dark and exceedingly handsome. He said he came from Pakistan and had been studying in England for two years. His name was Shalid, and his father was a director of railways. He himself was going to be an electronics engineer. He had, alas, no motor vehicle just at present, but perhaps nonetheless Val would do him the honor of going out with him one day? Maybe Saturday, for instance?

Val, smiling one of the veiled smiles which she reserved for such occasions, said she would have to think about it. Shalid said he begged that she would and then, as if noticing Maggie for the first time, carelessly added the information that he had a friend called Abdul, who was also at the college.

"If we are all of us going together, we are making up a foursome, isn't it?"

Val smiled again and said: "We'll let you know."

"You will be here tomorrow? At the same table?"

Val said that they might be.

"Then I will bring my friend."

"Do," said Val. "After all"—she dug her spoon into her yogurt, waiting until Shalid was out of earshot—"if the friend is too hideous for words, we can easily think up an excuse."

It was Maggie's experience that the friends of handsome young men were always too hideous for words, but it wouldn't be the first time she had suffered in the line of duty.

After lunch they had English with a lady in chiffon scarves called Mrs. Huxtable. She gave them typed lists of words, like "received" and "desiccated," which she said were commonly misspelled and they would do well to memorize, and then she made them write down "Dear Sirs—Yours faithfully" and "Dear Mr. Blank—Yours sincerely" and "Messrs. Smith & Brown BUT NEVER WITH LIMITED." Maggie, obediently writing, felt her neck break out in a flush. If Pa were here, how he would roar—except that it wouldn't be with laughter. "Is that what you've spent the last twelve years at school for?"

Mrs. Huxtable said she was going to read out an example of what a business letter ought not to be. She read: "Dear Sirs, We are in receipt of yours of the 25th ult.—" and then she stopped and said: "I take it there is no one who doesn't know what 'ult.' is intended to mean?" Silence. "In that case, would someone care to tell me?"

More silence. "Well, Miss Easter? Surely you ought to know?"

Maggie's neck broke out again, resentfully. Why should she know? She was science, not languages.

"I can't believe that a person with three A-levels—"

The rest of the class turned to look at her. Defiantly she muttered: "Ultimo."

"Meaning?"

"Last."

"And in this context, last month. Precisely. Why couldn't you have said so?"

Maggie buried her head in her book. If she was going to have those blasted A-levels cast up at her every time a question needed answering—

"No false modesty," said Mrs. Huxtable. "If you know a thing, say so."

Happily, when it came to office practice, she didn't know anything at all and could be as dim as she liked. Just because you'd got three A-levels hanging about your neck like an albatross—if albatrosses did hang about necks—it didn't mean that you were necessarily expected to be intimate with the workings of a duplicator or able to operate a Xerox machine. She managed to ruin more than a dozen sheets of photocopy paper before Miss Everton came flying to the rescue (of the machine, rather than her).

"Really, Miss Easter! How can you be so stupid?"

At the time she took an almost perverse delight in it. It was only later that, thinking back over the events of the day, she felt ashamed. Pa always said: "If you're going to bother doing anything, do it properly." It wasn't clever to be stupid, not even at office practice.

On her way back from college she stopped at the supermarket to buy supper. Fish and chips from the fish shop called to her rather strongly, but her calorie book showed a big black blob, which ruled it out, so instead she bought a can of Irish stew and a pound of potatoes. Even Val couldn't complain about a few measly potatoes after ham salad and yogurt for lunch.

It was as she was going up the front steps that she met Sebastian—if meeting him it could be called when not a word passed between them. Of course, at that stage she didn't actually know that he *was* Sebastian. He might equally well have been Mick Waters or the male half of Mr. and Mrs. Grace. He certainly didn't impress her as being anyone who could ever play an important part in her life. He went leaping up the steps before her, long and lanky. He was wearing a lumber jacket and jeans and mud-caked boots, obviously home from work. The town was full of building sites; she dismissed him as just a laborer. (It only went to show, as she thought afterward, the horrors of a middle-class upbringing: *just a laborer.* Echoes of Ma.)

At the top of the steps he paused, fractionally, to hold the door for her. His face was rather too thin, all caverns and shadows, with big, dark, deep-set eyes and limp black hair, which fell over his forehead, and that was really about as much as she noticed. She didn't have time to notice any more because the next second he was off, bounding up the stairs three at a time before she could even say "thank you," never mind introduce herself.

When the others heard of it later, they said: "Yes, well, that's Sebastian for you . . . mad as a flaming hatter."

5

The following evening Val came back to Station Road
with her, and a bit later on Chris dropped by, and they
all had chicken curry from the Indian takeout place on
the corner. They were just picking over the bones—Chris
and Maggie were picking over the bones; Val was saying:
"Honestly. I don't know how you *can"*—when there was a
knock at the door and a girl was standing there. Maggie
knew, even before she announced herself, that she was
Paula Rose. She had to be. Her hair was a frizzy mop,
bright carrot color, her dress looked as if it had been
found on a rubbish dump, circa 1900, her feet were bare,
with toenails painted scarlet, and on every finger of each
hand she wore a ring, or even two or three.

Maggie gazed at her in silent awe, not unmixed with
envy. It was the sort of getup Val wouldn't have been
seen dead in. Indeed, on Val it would have looked like a
mess because Val was essentially a very neat and ordered
person. On Paula Rose it looked exactly right.

She had come to ask Maggie if she might retrieve half
a pound of butter which had fallen onto Maggie's balcony from two floors above. Butter, it seemed, had a
habit of falling onto Maggie's balcony.

"We keep it on the kitchen window ledge. Sometimes it just goes splat. You may have noticed a sheet of plastic spread out there—that's because we got sick to death of eating bits of buttered balcony for breakfast."

("Why on the window ledge?" wondered Val later. "Keep it cool," said Maggie. There were some things Val just didn't know.)

They collected the butter, which was not soft enough to have gone splat, and Paula said how about them all coming up for a coffee—except that if they wanted it white, could they bring their own milk because she had forgotten to pick any up on her way home from work and they had only a few drops left.

"Don't you have it delivered?" said Val.

Paula looked at her vaguely. "I never thought about it."

Maggie hadn't thought about it either. She took her already opened carton, and they all went upstairs to the third floor, where in the middle of a large, untidy room, with unmade bed and empty beer cans crowding out the hearth, a boy wearing nothing but a pair of purple underpants was sitting on top of a television set, hacking at his toenails with what looked like garden shears. His hair, very long and blond, was pulled back into an elastic band. (Just as well Dot hadn't encountered *him* on the stairs.) As the door opened, he glanced around and, catching sight of Chris, threw both arms in the air, garden shears along with them, and shouted incomprehensibly: "Navycake, you big baboon!"

From somewhere in the vicinity of Maggie's left ear came her brother's voice in cordial response: "Navycake yourself, you great gorilla!"

Val, being more accustomed to the ways of boyfriends

than the ways of brothers, widened her eyes in astonishment. Maggie, having been brought up with the ways of
brothers (and the ways of Chris in particular), simply
clutched more tightly at her carton of milk: after the exchange of insults, the exchange of blows.

Thump. Punch. Wallop.

Paula looked at Maggie and said: "School?"

She pulled a face. "I guess."

She vaguely recalled, now, that there had been a blond
boy who used to come to Chris's parties. His hair in
those days had reached only as far as his shoulders, but
she remembered Pa's sarcastically inquiring of Chris, one
morning at the breakfast table, what color hairnet his
friend wore for rugby. It was undoubtedly the same boy.
Paula groaned and jerked at the door.

"I'm going to make the coffee . . . coming?"

Val and Maggie both followed her.

"It's the one thing that gets me about this place . . .
can't move an inch without tripping over someone
you've been to school with."

Val nodded, wisely. "That's why we're getting out."

"Soon as we've qualified."

"Going to the States."

"Doing what?" Paula plonked the kettle on the gas.

"Shorthand-typing," said Maggie.

Val sent her one of her looks. "Secretarial," she said.

She'd told her about that before. It was a secretarial
course they were taking, not shorthand-typing. Maggie
wasn't quite sure even now that she knew what the difference was. Something to do with status, according to
Val.

"She's a shorthand-typist downstairs," said Paula.
"Have you met her?"

"The girl who wears brown?"

"Sandy Grace—she's not bad. A bit wholesome. Works in a bank."

Maggie wondered why the information should depress her. What did it matter to her what Sandy Grace did? Not everyone who was a shorthand-typist had to be wholesome and work in a bank.

"What do you do?" said Val.

Paula was a sales assistant in a shop called Odds & Sods in the High Street. She said she was surprised they had never seen her in there.

"I don't think we've ever been in," said Val.

That surprised her even more. She said the gear was "absolutely fabulous, and dirt cheap with it . . . dress like this for next to nothing, would you believe?"

Val made a noise in the back of her throat. Maggie said hastily: "What about Mick? What does he do?"

"That," said Paula, "is one of those questions best left unanswered. He's got five old cars in a dump down by the railway, and every now and again he takes them to pieces and puts them back together again, and once in every blue moon he actually makes one of them go. . . . He's what's known as a mechanical genius; I'm what's known as the main breadwinner. He says it's women's lib."

Val rolled her eyes. She wasn't too keen on women's lib at the best of times. She liked to be treated like a lady, did Val.

"How about the boys on the ground floor?" said Maggie.

"Peter and Jimmy? Peter's a teacher. He's nice. Jimmy does things with computers. He's okay so long as you watch your step. He's into this really heavy scene at the moment . . . black consciousness and all that."

"People who are 'into' things," said Val, "tend to be an awful drag."

"I wouldn't say Jimmy was a drag. He just tends to get a bit touchy."

"I wonder how he'd feel if we went to his country and got a bit touchy."

Maggie frowned. She wished Val wouldn't come out with remarks like that. They made her feel uncomfortable.

"I'll take the coffee in," she said.

Mick and Chris were sitting on cushions on the floor. The bed was still unmade, but as a concession to company Mick had clad his lower half in a pair of what appeared to be pajama trousers and his upper half in a sweat shirt with SWEET DREAMS written across the front of it. They had obviously been indulging in a what-a-small-world-it-is session. As Maggie set down the tray with its five assorted mugs, she heard Mick say: "Yeah, and I'll tell you who else is living here . . . Sebastian."

"What! Not your actual Brains?"

"Your actual Brains. In person, no less."

"You're kidding!" Chris choked, then laughed. It was a laugh that contained more of derision than affection. "That maniac!"

Really, thought Maggie. Whoever said that men weren't capable of being catty? She helped herself to a handleless blue mug with pink elephants dancing trunk to tail all the way around the outside of it and drew up a cushion. Val and Paula sat on the unmade bed. The floor show began; it was utterly predictable.

"Presenting, for your delectation—"

"For one week only—"

"By special request—"

"The actual and original—"

"One and only—"

"And truly unique—"

"Sebastian . . . Sutton!"

Hoots, jeers, and hunting noises. Loud raspberry, followed by coarse cackle. Such little things amused them. Maggie regarded them darkly over the rim of her mug.

"Tautology," she said.

They ignored that. Probably didn't know what the word meant. Chris hadn't even learned to read until he was nine. It was Paula who leaned forward and said: "You what?"

"Tautology," said Maggie. "If he's the one and only, then he's got to be unique, and if he's unique, he doesn't need qualifying."

"You can say that again," said Mick.

"But what's he doing here?" Chris stretched out for a mug with a large chunk missing from the rim, which Val had studiously avoided. "I thought the genius had got himself to Oxford?"

"Cambridge. Yeah. He got there."

"So what's he doing down here?"

"Humping the humble hod."

"Eh?"

"On the buildings."

"Oh!" Light dawned. "Vacation job?"

"Nope. Been at it the last few months."

"So what happened to Cambridge?"

"Dunno. Never talks about it."

A wrinkle of exasperation creased Chris's forehead.

"You're never telling me the great steaming nit got himself chucked out of there as well?"

Mick humped a shoulder. "So who'd be surprised?"

"But how could even that pathetic lunatic—"

"He probably failed his exams," said Paula. She looked rather hard at Mick. "Some of us do—and then, on the whole, we'd rather *not* have to talk about it."

They shook their heads, very definite.

"Not Brains."

"Not unless he screwed it up on purpose."

"Which, of course, is always possible."

Val leaned down from the bed and deposited her mug of coffee, half-finished, on the tray.

"Does one gather he was thrown out of somewhere else?"

"School," said Mick. "Got the shove."

"Bootsie put the boot in."

" 'If ever I catch you skulking around these premises again—' "

Oh, hilarity, thought Maggie. She thought of the long, lanky boy with the too thin face and deep dark eyes, leaping up the steps ahead of her in his lumber jacket and mud-caked boots. That presumably had been Sebastian. She felt suddenly sorry for him.

"What on earth did he do?" said Val. Boys at Tennyson had been expelled from time to time, but that was mostly for clobbering the staff or persistent defacing of school property. They didn't behave like that at Trinity. Trinity was minor public; it took only "nice" boys.

"What did he *do?*" said Mick. "What *didn't* he do? Remember that time he climbed up onto the roof and wouldn't come down?"

"And that other time when he locked himself in the can and refused to come out?"

"Is he unbalanced?" said Val.

"Nutty as a fruitcake."

"But what did he do it for?" said Maggie. "He must have had a reason."

"Oh, he was demonstrating about something. Animal rights or something. Remember that time he got in the lab and let all the mice out?"

"Lord, yes! Old Lockjaw went balmy!"

"Not surprised—we were supposed to be dissecting 'em."

"And what about the frogs? Remember the frogs? Got all over the bloody place."

"That was when he started off on his vegetarian kick. Said we all ought to eat sunflower seeds."

"And he went and lectured the cook? Remember that? Told her she was aiding and abetting the slaughter of dumb animals . . . she whacked him around the head with a soup ladle!"

Both boys doubled up over their coffee mugs. Maggie said: "I don't see what's so funny about it. I don't see anything funny in wanting to stop animals being slaughtered."

Chris gasped.

"What's funny . . . is that his old man . . . is a farmer!"

Mick roared. Chris held his sides.

"Bloody farmer . . . slaughters everything within sight!"

Mirth. Even Val was permitting herself a slight smile, and Val's sense of humor was notoriously deficient. Personally Maggie still couldn't see anything to laugh about.

On the contrary, she thought it must have made life exceedingly uncomfortable for Sebastian, trying to be a vegetarian and having to watch his own father killing animals right and left.

"I suppose he's anti blood sports?" said Val.

"Anti everything. You name it, he's agin it."

"Money—"

"Profit—"

"Capital—"

"Didn't he once say your old man was a bloated capitalist exploiter?"

"Yeah, but he said his own was a bloody butcher."

"And property is theft."

"And property is theft. Oh, yes. Definitely. Property is a very dirty word. Only reason he's working on this site is because it's for an old people's home. If it was a bank, he wouldn't soil his hands."

Well, thought Maggie, that was reasonable. Sebastian was evidently a person with principles and stuck to them.

"You still haven't told us," said Paula, "what the poor mutt did to get the sack."

"Oh, he only stood up in the middle of morning assembly and told the Boot he was a fascist thug, didn't he?"

Paula giggled. "The Boot being your headmaster?"

"The Boot being our revered headmaster."

Really, it had to be said, there was something rather splendid about it. Maggie tried to imagine standing up before the whole school and informing Miss Stanhope that she was a fascist thug. The mere idea was enough to send pleasurable shivers down her spine.

"And was he?" said Paula.

"Oh, he was a thug, all right—the way he used to lay into us. Don't know about the other. Just because a guy chooses to invite some cruddy company director to come and jaw on Speech Day, I wouldn't have thought it automatically labeled him as a fascist."

"Especially," said Mick, "when it was a distinguished old boy. Only one the place has ever produced."

"Quite. Wasn't the Boot's fault the bloke turned out to be some kind of neo-Nazi."

"But he must have known," said Maggie.

They looked at her.

"What?"

"Mr. Wellington. Before he invited him. He must have known what the man was like."

"Oh!"

They weren't interested in that. That wasn't part of the story. The story was for ridiculing Sebastian, not debating moral issues. Maggie, however, could be stubborn.

"If Sebastian knew, then *he* must have known. And if the man was what you say he was, then he oughtn't to have invited him."

"Look, he wasn't actually a card-carrying member—"

"Just happened to have business interests in some part of the world where he shouldn't."

"You mean he exploited native labor?"

"Well—yes, if you like."

"And Sebastian was the only one to make a protest?"

Chris twitched an eyebrow rather irritably. "There are ways and ways of making protests."

"Did you make one?"

"Me? You must be joking! I was up to my neck in exams. What did I care who came and jawed? I didn't even know. Could have been a member of the KGB, for all I was aware."

"Are you saying Sebastian didn't tell you? Are you saying he didn't *canvass* you?"

"Oh, he mouthed! He's always mouthing."

"That's no excuse. Don't try to wriggle out of it."

"I'm not trying to wriggle out of it!"

"Yes, you are! You know you are! You turned a blind eye. I think Sebastian was quite right to make a stand. He obviously had more guts than the rest of you. Seems to me the rest of you were nothing but a load of lily-livered cowards."

Mick was staring at her, as if in fascination. Paula was grinning. Val was studying her nails. Chris said: "All right! All right! What would you have done? Be honest!"

Being honest, she said: "I probably wouldn't have stood up the way he did. But I might at least have got up a petition or something."

"So that's what I said: There are ways and ways of doing these things. You don't have to make a flaming exhibition of yourself."

Maggie was about to point out that it was better to make an exhibition of oneself than sit back and do nothing when it struck her that they were going in circles and if she pushed it any further, she would only make herself unpopular. Chris would groan and say: "Here we go," and Val would lecture her afterward about being aggressive. She contented herself instead, therefore, with muttering: "Anyway, wasn't Sebastian up to *his* neck?"

"He sure was afterward," said Mick.

Chris scowled and said: "Shut up talking about Sebastian. He bores me."

"You were the ones that brought the subject up," said Maggie. "I'd never even heard of him."

"Well, now you have, so who's a lucky girl?"

She had touched him on a sore spot. In spite of all his protestations, he felt guilty about having left Sebastian to bear the responsibility. It was one of Pa's maxims that moral cowardice was more heinous than physical.

"You don't think he's the boy you met yesterday?" said Val.

"Probably." She didn't want to talk about yesterday. She wished now she had never mentioned it to Val in the first place. She hadn't known then, of course, who Sebastian was. She had thought he was "just a laborer."

Val turned eagerly to the others. "She met this peculiar boy who wouldn't talk to her. Just turned tail and bolted."

"Yeah, well, that's Sebastian for you: mad as a flaming hatter."

Val said: "Is he on drugs? It sounds to me as if he might be."

Oh? And what, pray, did Val know about it?

"Sebastian doesn't need to be on drugs," said Mick. "He lives on a permanent high of his own."

"When he's not being a manic-depressive. I tell you, he's raving. Just shut *up* about him."

They didn't mention Sebastian again for the rest of the evening. At half past eleven, when they were reluctantly thinking of making a move, Mick said: "When are you returning to your northern fastness?"

"Some time Sunday. Depends when I can get a lift."

"Good. Means you'll be here for the party."

"Party?" said Paula. "Are we having a party?"

"Saturday night. Why not? Introduce Maggie to the

rest of the house. How about it?" He turned to Maggie. "On?"

She exchanged glances with Val, who said: "Can we bring someone?" (At lunch that morning Shalid had duly presented his friend Abdul for inspection. As friends went, he had not been too hideous. At any rate, Maggie had been lumbered with far worse.)

Mick said: "Sure. Bring who you like. The more the merrier."

"Jimmy will turn up with a whole harem," said Paula. "He always does. . . . I suppose we shall have to ask Them Downstairs?"

"We shall if we don't want them complaining about noise. It's all right, they won't stay."

"What about Sebastian?" said Maggie. "Are you going to invite him?"

Chris groaned. Mick looked doubtful. Paula said: "Yes, of course we are. How could we not? If we can put up with Them Downstairs, we can certainly put up with Sebastian."

Maggie's heart warmed to her.

"I don't know what you've both got against him," said Paula. "I know he can be a bit tiresome, but it's not as if there's any harm in him. *He* doesn't go around jeering at people behind their backs."

"Get her!" said Mick.

"Don't think she's gone and fallen for him, do you?"

"For *Sebastian?*"

They collapsed.

"As a matter of fact," said Paula, "there are *moments* when I'm quite fond of him. There are other moments, admittedly, when I feel like knotting a pair of tights around his neck, but that's no more than I feel ninety

percent of the time with you, you great sniggering oaf."
She looked at Maggie and shook her head. "Never get
yourself tied up with a man," she said.

"No! Try Sebastian instead!"

The guffawing could have been heard several blocks
away.

6

There were good parties, and there were bad parties. Mick and Paula's party was definitely one of the good ones. The room was crowded, bodies spilling out onto the stairs and into the kitchen. The hi-fi was turned up to full volume, the speakers pumping out reggae from a stack of records belonging to the boys on the ground floor: Peter, tall, bespectacled, rather earnest; Jimmy, with his promised harem, brash and bouncy, more of an extrovert.

Val was there, in a black chiffon blouse and slinky satin trousers which hugged her hips and which on anyone else would have revealed nasty little rolls of fat. With Val, even if you stole a sly glance at her sideways when she wasn't expecting it, her stomach still remained as flat as a pancake.

Shalid and Abdul were there, Shalid looking romantic, like the sheikh of Araby, Abdul looking longingly at Val. Maggie was too used to it to be insulted. Whenever they made up a foursome, Val was always the center of attraction. She only thought that perhaps in this case he might have tried to be a little less obvious about it.

Chris turned up with another ex-school friend (more

cries of "Navycake!"; more thumps and wallops) whom
he introduced as Baz, plus two females, whom he introduced as Baz's sister and Baz's cousin. He was clad in his
most ghastly pair of jeans, all frayed and faded and
patched, together with one of Dot's special chunky hand
knits that Maggie couldn't wear. Alone of all the family,
Maggie had had the misfortune to take after Grandpa
Easter. Grandpa Easter was what Jesse called a typical
pyknic, which as a child Maggie had thought must have
something to do with eating, but apparently not. It came
from the Greek word *pyknos* and meant that as a type you
were shortish and stockyish with a roundish sort of face.
Jesse said that Maggie was a female pyknic and, being so,
looked like nothing so much as a beach ball when en-
veloped in the folds of one of Dot's chunky sweaters.
Chris could get away with it. He wasn't very tall, but no
one could accuse him of looking like a beach ball. In fact,
in spite of the jeans, she wasn't actually ashamed to have
him for a brother.

The Graces arrived, bearing a bottle of white wine,
which added a touch of class since everyone else had
brought common or garden beer or cider. Sandy was still
wearing brown; perhaps that was why she was called
Sandy. Perhaps she never wore anything else. Her husband's name Maggie did not discover. She only ever re-
ferred to him as "my husband," and somehow there
wasn't the opportunity to ask. (Or was it simply that she
couldn't summon up enough interest?) He had discarded
his suit but still had an air of formality; he was the only
man in the room wearing a collar and tie.

Sebastian came by himself. For all their gibes, he
looked quite sane—saner, one would have said, than
Mick, whose blond hair was now hanging loose, con-

fined by only a sweat band, whose T-shirt was embla-
zoned with words unmentionable, and whose pajama
bottoms had been replaced by a pair of shiny plastic
trousers (doubtless got for a song from Odds & Sods).
Sebastian's clothing was at least conventional. His
sweater might have holes at the elbows, but his jeans
were a sight less revolting than Chris's.

There were no cries of "Navycake!" when Sebastian
entered the room. Chris shouted, "Ah: begorrah"—one
had to shout, to make oneself heard—" 'tis the one an'
only!"

Baz bellowed: "Hi, there, Brains! Hear you got yourself a prole job?" Watching them, Maggie had the feeling
that neither of them was quite comfortable.

"Meet m'sister." Chris stretched out an arm and
hauled her in. "She says you ignored her on the stairs the
other night."

"No, I did not!" She wrenched herself free indignantly.
"I said we never got around to introducing ourselves."

"So now's your chance . . . Maggie, meet Sebastian
—otherwise known as Brains. Sebastian, m'sister Maggie."

Sebastian said: "Hello, Sister Maggie."

Maggie held out her hand and said: "Hello."

Sebastian's handshake was surprisingly firm. Somehow, with one so long and lanky, she had expected it to
be limp. Limp and a bit damp, but it wasn't either.

"You can call him Brains," shouted Chris. "He won't
mind."

"I'd rather call him Sebastian, thank you," said Maggie. "I like the name Sebastian."

"Do you really?" Sebastian sounded surprised. "I always think it conjures up images of effete youths with teddy bears."

"That's only because of *Brideshead.*"

"Brideshead?" bellowed Chris. "What's Brideshead?"

"Brideshead Revisited, you idiot! Name of a book by Evelyn Waugh."

"Never heard of it."

"No, well, you always were illiterate."

Chris shouted: "Such a sweet girl . . . you haven't by any chance *got* a teddy bear, have you, Brains?"

"Three!" yelled Sebastian.

"What?"

"I said, I've got three . . . they're my greatest passion in life."

Chris staggered and clutched at Maggie. "Don't tell me! You take them all to bed with you?"

"Of course! You wouldn't expect me to leave them outside in the cold, would you?"

Chris said: "Spare me!"

"They have their feelings, you know, the same as everyone else."

Chris choked. Baz shouted: "Does 'oo cuddle all a lickle bears 'en?"

"Naturally!" bawled Sebastian. "Bears need a great deal of cuddling."

He kept such a straight face that Maggie wondered for one startled moment whether he really meant it. She had to shake herself before she realized that of course he didn't—that of course he couldn't. No boy of nineteen went to bed with three teddy bears. He was just putting them on, playing them at their own game. Wasn't he?

Baz, enjoying himself, bellowed: "So does all a lickle

teddy bears have 'ickle names 'en? What does 'oo call all a lickle teddy bears?"

Sebastian's reply came without so much as a flicker of hesitation. "Humpty, Dumpty, and Franklin D."

"I don't believe it!"

(Strange, thought Maggie, how easily hoodwinked some people were.)

In a sudden lull, unexpectedly, Baz's sister entered the conversation. "Baz had a teddy bear once. He called it Tholly, short for Tholomon."

"He mutht have had a lickle lithp," said Sebastian.

"One does," said Baz, "when one is only three years old."

"One hopes," said Chris, "to have grown out of these things by the time one reaches puberty." He tapped Sebastian on the chest. "So what happened to Cambridge, you great nana?"

"Cambridge?"

Sebastian's eyes slid away. Maggie saw his fingers tighten their grip on the obligatory bottle that he had brought with him.

"Big seat much learning. City of dreaming spires and what-have-you," said Chris.

Sebastian looked at him vaguely. "Oxford," he muttered.

"What?"

"He means the spires," said Maggie. "Dreaming spires . . . they're Oxford."

"Are they? I thought they were Cambridge."

"Well, they're not." And anyway, how tactless could you get? Asking someone about a place he'd been thrown out of. What business was it of Chris's? She saw him opening his mouth for another onslaught, and leaped in ahead. "Oxford has the spires, Cambridge has the fens . . . probably the reason why they never smile."

Sidetracked, Chris said: "What do you mean, never smile?"

" 'For Cambridge people rarely smile,
Being urban, squat, and packed with guile;
And Royston men in the far South
Are black and fierce and strange of mouth; . . .
But Grantchester! ah, Grantchester!
There's peace and holy quiet there . . .' "

Sebastian put up a hand and pushed a lock of hair out of his eyes. " 'Scuse me. Must go dump this bottle."

They watched as he wove his way through the crush of bodies to the drinks table in the far corner. Chris made a noise of disgust.

"I told you he was raving," he said.

If Sebastian was raving, thought Maggie, then Chris was an insensitive oaf. But then that was something she already knew. She had yet to be convinced there was anything amiss with Sebastian.

She didn't really have the opportunity to talk to him again—not that one could, above the noise of the hi-fi. She saw him wandering about, glass in hand, but their paths didn't cross. She watched as he moved from one knot of people to the next. She noticed that he would stay but a short while with each, hovering, as it were, on the outskirts, never quite one of the group, before moving on again. He seemed generally unattached, unable to make contact. She wondered, since they had now been formally introduced—and since Abdul could scarcely be

said to be guarding her with any degree of jealousy—
why he hadn't headed in her direction. She thought for a
while that maybe he was deliberately avoiding her, on
account of her being Chris's sister (she wouldn't have
blamed him; Chris could be piglike at times), but then
suddenly she found him at her side, holding out a hand
and saying: "Come and dance?" which made her think
that perhaps he didn't mind about her being Chris's sister after all.

Sebastian danced wildly, arms and legs flying off at
tangents, all independent of the others, like a puppet
gone out of control. At least he was not inhibited. People
like Val and Shalid went in for nothing more strenuous
than gentle gyrations; anything else made you sweat and
wasn't dignified. She liked Sebastian for his unashamed
cavortings. She had never much cared for dignity.

She might have sat on the floor with him, afterward,
and talked—or at any rate, mouthed and lip-read—but
Chris, annoyingly, came and dragged her away to "speak
to Baz's cousin . . . she's secretary to some big noise in
industry. She'll be able to tell you what it's all about."
She didn't particularly want to know what it was all
about, being secretary to some big noise, either in industry or in anything else, but since Baz's cousin was within
lip-reading distance, she hardly liked to say so. Fortunately Val saved the day by joining them and showing
the proper amount of interest—asking the sorts of intel-
ligent questions that would never have occurred to Maggie, such as "Does he let you write your own letters?"
and "Does he ever take you to conferences with him?"—
so that Maggie had only to nod and smile and make the
occasional grunting sound.

Sebastian, after she had been dragged away from him,

sat on the floor by himself, with his knees drawn into his chest and his arms wrapped around them. He sat immobile, and people moved around him as if he were a piece of the furniture. The holes in his elbows showed very clearly.

It didn't seem right, at a party, that someone should be left to sit by himself. Maggie kept wanting to go over and sit with him, but every time she made a move she was buttonholed by someone. Finally, she looked around, and he had gone. Paula was yelling at Mick across the room to "turn the volume down, there's been complaints." The sudden drop in noise level was almost deafening.

"What's happened to old Simple Simon?" said Chris. "Has he left?"

"He's gone for a walk."

"At this time of night?"

"He said he was going to go over the marsh and gaze at the water."

Groans.

"With a view to throwing himself in?"

"Either that, or exposing himself in the bushes."

More groans. Paula rooted among the debris of bottles for one which might still have something in it.

"He hadn't yet made up his mind—What creep dunked a cigarette end in the cider?"

Loud chorus of disclaimers.

"Not me!"

"Don't smoke."

"Well, some creep is responsible."

Baz's cousin, who had drunk more beer than was good for her, suddenly giggled and said: "I say, you don't think he would?"

"Would what?"

"What he said—"

"Oh! Who knows?" Paula was plainly more interested in fishing the cigarette end out of the cider than in worrying her head about Sebastian. "Never be surprised what he might not get up to. He's zany enough."

"Tell you one thing," said Chris. "He needn't think I'm going down to the cop shop to bail him out."

Guffaws all around. How too hilarious! Maggie wondered why it was they all seemed to think it funny and she did not. Sometimes it was as if she weren't quite switched onto the same wavelength.

Val, who by now had reached the stage of lounging on Shalid's lap (naturally on the room's one and only armchair), said: "Do you think Sebastian is quite normal?"

"Sebastian," said Jimmy, "is a pain."

"Yes, but is he *normal?*"

"Of course he's not normal! He's raving bloody bananas."

"He's normal in that way," said Paula.

Mick spun around to look at her.

"How do you know?"

"One knows, that's how I know."

"You ever seen him with a girl?"

"No, but that's nothing to go by."

"Then how do you know?"

"I told you . . . one has an instinct."

"Huh!"

"It doesn't sound to me as if he's very normal," said Val. "Saying things like that."

"Oh! Sebastian just says things for effect. He doesn't mean anything by them. He just likes to try it on. Thinks he might be shocking you."

"Anything to draw attention to himself."

"What's known as an exhibitionist."

"And how!"

"Remember that time at school he threatened to pour gasoline over himself?"

"Yeah, and what about that other time—"

They were at it again. Balmy Sebastian; crazy Sebastian. Sebastian is a pain, is a bore, is a raving bloody nut.

Maggie shot a quick glance about the room. Val and Shalid had their lips glued together like a pair of goldfish; Abdul was trying to make out with one of Jimmy's harem; Chris had his nose buried inches deep in a beer mug. No one was likely to miss her. Swiftly she rose to her feet, slipped out through the door and down the stairs.

Across the road was a footpath leading to the marsh. The marsh was one of those places that by day were utterly dismal—a mile and a half of dank wasteland, with abandoned cars and shattered television sets dumped all the way around the perimeter, and in the middle a pool of deep, dark, weed-choked water, with the occasional solitary sea gull swooping over the surface. At night, with the bare, bleak landscape silvered by the moon, and the monster bulks of the bellying gasholders lumbering like prehistoric predators over the horizon, it changed and became sinister. Maggie was hardly the girl to be scared by shadows, but she would not normally have walked the marsh alone.

It was a relief to see Sebastian—as she did almost at once. His lanky form, silhouetted against the skyline, was unmistakable. He was leaning against the mutilated trunk of a weeping willow, split asunder in a storm of years gone by, staring down into the dark depths of the pool. He didn't glance around as Maggie approached. He didn't jump or seem in any way startled as her feet scrunched on the frosty grass. For a long while they stood in silence, Sebastian with his arms hanging limply by his sides, Maggie with both hands thrust into the back pockets of her jeans. Then Sebastian, without taking his eyes off the water, said: "Have you ever thought of drowning yourself?"

She supposed he must have been waiting for someone to come after him just so that he could say it. Briskly she said: "No. Have you?"

"Yes."

Just for a second she was thrown. Had he said: "Frequently!" or "I do it all the time"—something flip, something camp—she would have known how to cope. Cool but jokey, to show she wasn't impressed. The simple monosyllable took her aback. But of course, it was meant to, wasn't it? "Likes to think he might be shocking you." Well, he needn't think he was shocking *her.* Maggie Easter wasn't shockable.

Dryly, in her best imitation of Pa at his most squashing, she said: "You make a habit of it, I suppose?"

"Only sometimes."

"You must have an Ophelia complex."

He frowned. "Ophelia was mad."

"Well—yes." She was, of course. There could be no denying it. "Mind you, I reckon she had enough to make her . . . what with old Ham sending her off to be a nun and practically never stopping talking from one end of the play to the other. Keeping on about death all the time. It must have been pretty gruesome for her."

"Life is pretty gruesome."

"Not enough to drown oneself."

"Why? What would be so awful about it? I read somewhere that it was warm and comforting, like a cloak."

She was about to say: "Warm and *com*forting?" when
she stopped herself. This was all wrong. She was only
encouraging him. If she let him carry on in this vein, he
would begin to think he was impressing her, which he
quite definitely was *not.*

"Well, I don't know where you read that," she said,
"but if you ask me it's far more likely to be cold and wet
. . . catch your death if you weren't very careful."

Ha-ha. That was a joke, in case he hadn't noticed. She
might as well not have bothered—Sebastian didn't even
smile. Instead, abruptly, still staring down at the water,
he said: "Can you swim?"

"Well enough," said Maggie, and instinctively she
backed away, just in case.

But Sebastian, with a sigh, only said: "Yes. So can I. It
would be easier if one couldn't."

"Oh, indubitably," said Maggie. *(They're right,* she
thought; *he's just a poseur.)*

"One would almost certainly start striking out even if
one didn't want to."

"Undoubtedly. Survival instinct."

"I don't know how strong one's willpower is."

"One could always try filling one's pockets with
bricks."

"Yes, I thought of that."

"Or maybe it would just be easier to swallow a bottle
of aspirin."

For the first time Sebastian turned to look at her. His
face in the moonlight was almost gaunt. He needed one
of Dot's three-course dinners.

"People who talk of it," he said, "never do it, do they?"

He made it sound as if it were a serious question.

"No," said Maggie. She said it very firmly. "People who talk of it don't."

"That's what I thought." He turned back to the water. "That's why I talk of it."

Maggie regarded him uncertainly. This was some kind of game they were playing, wasn't it? Or wasn't it?

"Why did you leave the party?" she said.

"Felt like being alone."

"Oh! Sorry, I'm sure. In that case I'll go back."

"Away from all the noise," said Sebastian. "Noise is very"—he put up a hand and pushed a lock of hair out of his eyes, a gesture she was already learning to recognize as characteristic—"very confusing," he said.

"Yes, I suppose it is," said Maggie, though, in fact, she never found it so.

"It makes kaleidoscopes in my brain. I can't concentrate."

"We had a teacher at school who said it helped if you built yourself a big black chimney and crawled into it. He said in exams, if people were coughing or there were planes going overhead, just crawl into your chimney and you wouldn't notice. It does work; I've tried it. Of course, I don't know about parties. I'm not really sure one goes to parties to concentrate. But I suppose if one wanted to shut off for just a minute or so—"

"It's all right now." Sebastian suddenly peeled himself away from his tree trunk. "I can think again." He jerked his head. "Come for a walk?"

It was chilly, walking over the marsh at one o'clock in the morning without any coat. Sebastian insisted on giving Maggie his sweater, the sleeves of which were so long she could pull them over her hands like mittens. She tried to argue against it because all he had on underneath was a thin shirt with most of the buttons missing, but Sebastian said he didn't feel the cold, and anyway, if you walked fast enough, you didn't need clothes to keep warm. Accordingly, they did a fast march across the marsh, Sebastian striding ahead, windmilling with his arms, Maggie doing little hops and skips to keep up.

"Let's play the poetry game," said Sebastian.

"What"—she did two quick hops—"is the poetry game?"

"What is the poetry game? The poetry game is the poetry game . . . like I might say, *'Remember me when I am gone. . . .'*"

"And I might say, *'I remember, I remember, the house where I was born'?*"

"And you might say, *'I remember, I remember, the house where I was born'* . . . and then I would say, *'A time to be born, and a time to die. . . .'*"

"*'If I should die, think only this of me. . . .'*"

Sebastian groaned.

"Brooke, Brooke! You have Brooke on the brain."

"It's poetry, isn't it?"

"If you say so . . . How about:

> *"Think no more; 'tis only thinking*
> *Lays lads underground."*

She did another hop.

"Is that Brooke?"

"No, it is not! It's Housman. *Shropshire Lad*. Go on, your turn."

They played the poetry game all the way across the

marsh and all the way back. Sebastian beat her hands down; his knowledge of poetry seemed encyclopedic. She wondered if it was English that he had been studying at the university but didn't like to ask. Chris had already been clubfooted enough for one day. Instead, trying to be cunning, she said: "It's not really fair. I was science, not languages," but he didn't take the bait.

He only pushed a lock of hair out of his eyes and said: "If more scientists read more poetry, the world might be a better place to live in."

As they walked up the front steps, the door opened, and Val and Shalid came out. Val gave Maggie a funny look and said: "Oh, there you are. We're just leaving. Abdul went some time ago; he had a train to catch."

"He is making his excuses," said Shalid.

Val tossed her head. "If you ask me," she said, "it's Maggie who ought to be making hers."

The door slammed behind her.

"Now I'm in the doghouse," said Maggie.

She was in the doghouse with more than just Val. When she arrived back upstairs (she tried to coax Sebastian, but he wouldn't come; he said he had some reading to do), she found Chris waiting for her with a face like the father of the gods about to hurl thunderbolts.

"Where the devil have you been?" he said.

She raised an eyebrow. "Out with Sebastian. We went for a walk over the marsh."

"Well, you shouldn't bloody well go for a walk over the marsh! For crying out loud! It's nearly two o'clock in the morning!"

"So what?"

"So you shouldn't go over the poxy marsh, that's what!"

"Look, I was with *Sebastian*—"

"Yes, and Sebastian is a bloody nut!"

She faced him angrily. "Do you have to keep saying that? Can't you for once in your life be just a little charitable?"

"I wouldn't feel very charitable if I found my own sister lying dead in a ditch with her throat cut."

"Oh, for heaven's *sake!* Don't be so stupid."

"Now you just listen to me, you! You weren't at school with the bloke. You don't know what a nut he is. You—"

"Will you stop *saying* that?"

"Children, children!" It was Mick, stationing himself between them. He wagged a finger. "No quarreling. Ain't worth it."

"Especially not over poxy Sebastian."

"Especially not over"—Mick caught Maggie's eye—"over Sebastian. Honest, Mags. Sebastian's a loner. Always has been."

"Yes, and it's no good thinking *you* can get through to him," said Chris, "because you can't. Nobody can."

She wondered, as she gave her brother one last venomous glare, how many people had ever really tried.

7

Maggie set her alarm for nine the following morning, even though it had been long past three o'clock before she had gone to bed. She had promised Dot most faithfully that she would be in Chislehurst in time for lunch, and "in time" to Dot always meant at least two hours earlier than it did to anyone else. Dutifully, after twice falling back to sleep, she managed to stagger out of bed into sweater and jeans and went stumbling down the stairs with her eyelids still glued together to buy the paper. Sunday morning, even in her own room, was unthinkable without the color supplement.

The rest of the house was in silence—everyone, she supposed, still sleeping off the effects of the party. There were no sounds of movement even from the Graces on the floor above, and they had left before midnight. She tiptoed down the hall ("Always consider your neighbors," Dot had said. It was no doubt good policy; she shuddered to think of Jimmy's reaction at being dragged from slumber by a great clumping female at half past nine on a Sunday morning) and, reaching the front door, with its stained-glass lily panel, carefully eased it open, remembering for once to keep hold of it so that it wouldn't bang.

As she stepped out into the dubious daylight of Station Road, filtered as always through a pall of car exhaust, a dark shape took a flying leap from the top of the steps. For a few desperate seconds the shape clung, scrabbling, to the wooden palings of the fence; then, giving up the struggle, it dropped into the flower bed and streaked belly to ground for the protection of the old yew tree in the corner. At Maggie's feet lay a moldering fish head, half-chewed. With a grimace, between finger and thumb, she picked it up. Instantly, from the yew tree, came a piteous cat cry.

"What's the matter?" said Maggie.

She walked over to the tree and stood looking up. The cat crouched on a branch, looking down. It was an exceedingly scrawny cat. It might have been pretty, with its gay patchwork coat and little round face, but its fur was harsh and matted, and she could see all its ribs sticking out.

"Is it yours? Are you hungry?" She held up the fish head. "Here you are, then—you can have it."

The cat backed away, along the branch.

"Well, come on!" said Maggie. "Take it if you want it."

The cat plainly did want it. It kept one eye upon the fish head, and one upon Maggie, but it wouldn't come take it from her. Every time she stretched up a hand, the cat would back a little farther away.

"So what do you want me to do?" said Maggie. "You want me to leave it for you?"

She placed the fish at the foot of the tree and went off across the road for her paper. When she came back, the fish was still there; so was the cat. At the sight of Maggie it gave another pitiful "miaa-ow!"

"Now what's the matter?"

What was the matter, it seemed, was that the cat had got itself stuck. In its panic it had fled too far and was now too scared to move either upward or down. Maggie clicked her tongue impatiently.

"Stupid idiot animal! Wait there."

She walked back up the steps and opened the front door. Hopefully she stood for a moment. No one. Not even Jimmy in a rage. With a sigh she dumped her paper and went back down. Yew trees, as she knew from experience, could be painful, and cats, as she knew from experience, could scratch. But she couldn't go off to Chislehurst and leave it there.

She was about to make the ascent when a voice from behind her said: "Hello, Sister Maggie! And what are you up to this fine day?"

She turned and saw Sebastian. He was wearing an old holey fisherman's knit sweater, so big and baggy that it came almost to his knees. His jeans were faded to the point of being practically colorless, and two bare toes poked through the gaps in his sneakers. With his chin unshaved and his hair uncombed, he looked a bit like a scarecrow, but quite a pleasant, friendly sort of scarecrow. She still didn't believe he was the raving lunatic they all made out.

"I'm rescuing a cat," she said.

"Rescuing a cat?" Sebastian stepped forward. "Where?"

She pointed. "Up there. It seems to have got itself stuck."

Sebastian looked up, into the tree. "She's not stuck, she's just scared . . . of you, probably."

"Oh." Maggie felt deflated. "Well, in that case—"

"Hang on," said Sebastian. "I'll get her."

The cat, it seemed, was not scared of Sebastian; at any rate, it didn't back away from him. Maggie saw his head disappearing into the branches of the yew tree. She heard his voice, coaxing: "Come on, then, puss . . . that's a girl! Down we go . . . slowly does it—" If that had been Chris, she thought, he would have said forget the poxy cat.

Inch by inch Sebastian reemerged. In his arms he held a submissive bundle of fur. Its eyes were big and its ears pulled back, but it was making no attempt to bite or scratch.

"I think it's hungry," said Maggie.

"She's more than hungry; she's half-starving."

"How do you know it's a she?"

"She's got teats—obviously had kittens. I'll bet some louse threw her out when he discovered she was pregnant. Just dumped her from a car and left her to get on with it. Chances are she's been living rough over the marsh."

"She must have followed us last night."

"Could have."

"What about the kittens?"

"Oh, they'll be dead. She won't have had enough milk. Poor little cow's half-dead herself."

"People are so foul," said Maggie.

"They do it all the time." Sebastian made a fold in his sweater and cuddled the cat in it. "We'll have to feed her. Have you got anything?"

"I've got some milk. She can have that."

"Milk's no good," said Sebastian. "She needs cream."

"Oh. Well—" Maggie felt in the pocket of her jeans. She still had the change from buying her paper. "I'll pop over the road and see if I can get some."

"See if you can get a bit of chicken as well."

"I'll try."

"Chicken or rabbit. One or the other."

"I'm not sure they sell it."

"Or fish would do, if you can't get meat."

"Except that if they don't sell meat," said Maggie, "they're not very likely to sell fish."

"Well, just so long as you don't go getting heart, or liver, or any of that sort of crap. It's got to be something that's easy to digest." Sebastian turned and walked back up the steps. "I'll see you inside. Don't be long."

Maggie pulled a face. "No, O master."

She came panting back within seconds, to find Sebastian sitting on the stairs outside her room, with the cat cradled in his arms.

"Did you get it?"

"I got the cream. They don't do fresh meat. I bought baby food—minced chicken. I thought if babies could digest it, a cat ought to be able to."

"Yeah, that should be okay," said Sebastian.

They took the cat into Maggie's room and fed her with her cream and her minced chicken.

"A bit at a time," said Sebastian. "She can have the rest later."

"I've got to go to Chislehurst later."

"Chislehurst?" Sebastian raised his head. He seemed to be searching for something. "You haven't got a soft brush or a—"

"To see my sister. Or a what?"

"Or a—" His eyes, roaming the room, came to rest on her hairbrush. "That would do."

"For what?"

"Brushing her. Can I have it?"

Resigned, she handed it to him. What was a hairbrush more or less? If it wasn't the hairbrush, it would only be something else.

She put the kettle on for coffee, took out two mugs, one cereal bowl, one spoon; hesitated; looked at Sebastian; took out another bowl, another spoon. He was obviously going to be staying for breakfast. She watched him as he brushed the cat with her hairbrush. His touch was firm and gentle; the cat was purring. It seemed he knew what he was doing when it came to animals.

She reached into the cupboard for the jar of instant.

"Do you take sugar in your coffee?"

"No, thank you."

"Milk?"

"No, thanks. She really ought to have a tray. We don't want her going outside again until she's stronger. I suppose you haven't got a—"

"No," said Maggie.

"How about this?" He had picked up an old Bakelite filing tray that Maggie had inherited from Pa and that was now doing service as a cutlery box. "This would do." He tipped it up, sending knives and forks scattering across the table. "Could be a bit deeper, but we can always stand it in the hearth."

"And what exactly are you going to put in it?"

"Ideally we need some cat litter. I don't suppose—"

"No."

"Well, shredded newsprint would do just as a temporary measure."

In the nick of time she whisked the Sunday paper out of reach.

"You can have the business section."

The cat watched the shredding operation with interest. The minute it was finished, she jumped into the box. Then she got out and began preening herself, emitting the occasional small chirrup as she did so. Sebastian, eating cornflakes, said: "Sign of a contented feline. So long as she's grooming, there can't be too much wrong with her." Maggie looked at her hairbrush full of cat's hairs and her cutlery box full of sodden newsprint.

"I'm glad someone's contented," she said.

It was two o'clock before she arrived in Chislehurst. Dot was agitated, thinking she'd forgotten.

"I rang to check, but they said you weren't there. I spoke to someone called Mick—I don't think he was properly awake. He mumbled something about a party. I couldn't make out what he was talking about. I didn't know whether you were on your way or whether you'd gone off somewhere else. I didn't know what to do about lunch. It's chicken casserole. I didn't know—"

"Ah!" said Maggie. "Chicken casserole!"

Chicken casserole would do nicely; it was the very thing.

She returned to Station Road, late in the evening, carrying the remains in a plastic fridge dish. She thought at first that she would take it up to Sebastian in the morning, but then she remembered that he was working on the buildings and had to leave at some hideous hour such as six o'clock, so that if the cat were to be fed before he went, she would need to take it up straightaway.

She hadn't seen Sebastian's room before, only passed

it en route to Mick and Paula's. It was tucked away on the half landing between the second and third floors, next door to the toilet and opposite the bath. It was smaller than Maggie's, and far more sparsely furnished— just a bed and a chair, one white wood cupboard, and a rickety table. Not even any proper cooking facilities. You couldn't do much, she would imagine, with one rusted gas ring. No wonder Sebastian was so thin: the result of not enough to eat.

He had obviously been in bed when she knocked, for he was wearing a pair of faded striped pajamas, rather too short in the arm and leg, as if they had been bought for him when he was much younger and he had grown out of them.

"Sorry," said Maggie. "Have I woken you?"

"No, it's all right, I was reading."

She saw now that there was a book lying open on the bed. (She squinted at it upside down. It looked like poetry—and all in French. Well, she supposed they didn't call him Brains for nothing.)

"I've brought some chicken for the cat's breakfast." She held out the plastic fridge pot. "Where is the cat?"

Sebastian grinned and pointed to a hump beneath the eiderdown. She was glad she knew it was the cat; she might otherwise have thought it was a teddy bear.

"Is she all right?"

"She will be. Just needs feeding up. I'll get her some proper cat litter tomorrow. If I leave my door unlocked, will you come and get her and put her into your room for the day? Give her more space to move about in."

"Do I take it"—Maggie hesitated—"that we're keeping her?"

"Well, I'm not handing her over to the RSPCA to be put to sleep."

"Surely they wouldn't?"

"They do if they can't find a home."

"Oh." In that case, it would seem there wasn't much alternative: 98 Station Road had acquired a cat. "What are we going to call her?" said Maggie.

"Sunday," said Sebastian. "On account of she's a Sunday cat."

8

Having Sunday to look after made a bond between them. Really and truly she was Sebastian's cat—she slept in his room at night, went out with him every morning, faithfully awaited his return on the gatepost in the evening—but Maggie nevertheless felt a certain responsibility toward her. She, after all, had been the one to find her, so it seemed only fair she should help with her upkeep. Not that she cost all that much. They halved the vet's bill for her vaccination against feline enteritis, which Sebastian insisted she should have as a precaution since there was no way of telling whether she had already had one or not, and at the end of October, when she was strong again, they were going to go halves on having her neutered, which Sebastian also insisted on. He said it was irresponsible to let female cats keep having litters willy-nilly all over the place.

Apart from the vet's bills, however, there was only her food, and really and truly one small cat didn't eat enough to break the bank. Maggie bought her ox heart from the butcher's: Sebastian bought her cat food from the supermarket. He wouldn't go into a butcher's. She had forgotten, until one day she asked him if he would mind doing

so because she wasn't going to have the time, and he said
no, he couldn't, it made him feel sick, that of course, he
was a vegetarian. It seemed he had no objection to the
cat's eating meat; it was human beings doing so that dis-
gusted him.

"Animals don't know any better; we're supposed to be
civilized."

Maggie, who was fond of her roast beef and two vege-
tables, said: "So long as they're allowed to have a good
life and are killed humanely, I don't see that there's anything wrong with it."

"Killed humanely!" Sebastian made an impatient,
scoffing sound. "Have you ever been around a slaughter-
house? Have you ever *watched* them? Have you ever seen
a herd of cows being shoved into a—"

"No," said Maggie. "But it's not as if they realize."

"Of course they realize! You think they're daft or
something?"

"Well, but they're only *animals.*"

"What d'you mean, they're only animals? So what?
They can still feel pain, can't they? Could *you* go out and
kill one?"

"Well, I—I wouldn't *want* to. Obviously."

"But you reckon you could? You reckon you could actually go out and slaughter a pig? You could actually cut
its throat and stand there watching while it bleeds to
death?"

"I could if I were starving."

"Yes, and what about if you weren't starving? Could
you then? You just think of it. . . . Think of a pig. All
pink and trusting. And you go out and clobber it just to
fill your gut—which could just as easily be filled with

something else. Why kill the poor bloody pig? It's got as much right to live as you."

She didn't argue the point; she wasn't sure that she could. It made her uncomfortable getting into this sort of discussion. She had already taken down her bullfight posters because Sebastian objected to them; she had no intention of changing her eating habits as well. All the same, it troubled her—the more so when she discovered that Sebastian actually went to the lengths of preaching what he practiced.

She and Val were shopping together in the square one Saturday morning when Val, distracted for a moment from the serious business of gazing into shopwindows, nudged Maggie in the ribs and said: "See what I see?" Maggie looked around, and there was Sebastian. He had taken up a stand in the main entrance, between the Communist *Morning Star* and the local Rotary Club, and had an armful of papers and a large white banner with the letters *VSP* printed on it in red capitals.

"Isn't it that weirdo from your place?" said Val.

Maggie frowned. She didn't like hearing Sebastian called a weirdo, and anyway, he wasn't. He might behave a trifle oddly when the fit was upon him, but in between he had quite long bouts of being just as normal as anyone else. He was eccentric, that was all.

"Go have a gander in Gear Change." She gave Val a little push toward a new boutique which someone had said did real silk stockings (Val having recently decided that stockings and garter belts were more sexy than tights). "I must just go see what he's up to."

What Sebastian was up to was selling newspapers. As he saw Maggie approaching, he held one out to her with a "Support the cause, lady?"

"Depends what it is." She nodded toward the banner. "What's *VSP* stand for?"

"Vegetarian Socialist Party."

"Vegetarian *Socialist* Party?"

"Yes. Why not? If you can have Christian Socialists, you can have vegetarian Socialists. Want one?"

She supposed that she would have to. It didn't seem as if many other people did.

"How much are they?"

"You can have the first one for free. I'll give you a sticker as well."

The sticker said "ANIMAL RIGHTS," and he had banged it onto the front of her sweater before she could stop him. (She felt a bit of an idiot walking around the square with "ANIMAL RIGHTS" plastered all over her chest, but out of loyalty to Sebastian she didn't like to peel it off.)

"How long have you been at it?" she said.

"Oh, about six months."

"I've never seen you."

"No, this is a new spot. I used to be down Coney Hill, outside Spatchley's. Police moved me on."

She wasn't surprised. Spatchley's was a large center where people went to stock up their freezers with sides of beef and lamb. They couldn't have been best pleased to have Sebastian standing outside every Saturday with his subversive vegetarian literature.

"You'll read it," he said, "won't you?"

She promised that she would, and did so over coffee while Val was busy admiring her new silk stockings and frilly red garter belt.

"Tights are awfully stuffy—especially the great thick things that most people wear. There's something *feminine* about stockings."

"Well, men would certainly look pretty silly in them," said Maggie.

Val drew her eyebrows together. She put the silk stockings back in their bag.

"What is that rubbish you're reading?"

"It's not rubbish." It might be a strange mixture—everything from SMASH THE GAFFERS to BAN THE BOMB and SAVE THE WHALE—but it definitely wasn't rubbish. "It's Sebastian's newspaper."

"Sebastian's newspaper! Load of rubbish."

Astounding how people like Val were always so ready to pass judgment. She hadn't even looked at the thing, never mind read it.

"I suppose before we know where we are, you'll be running around eating sunflower seeds."

"The day you take to nude bathing," said Maggie.

Just one of those smart-aleck remarks, at which her mother complained she was too clever by half.

"You'll get your comeuppance one of these days, my girl. You see if you don't."

She did—a fortnight later. It was entirely Sebastian's doing. She had gone up to see him partly to deliver some ox heart, partly to ask if he had a screwdriver she might borrow. He didn't answer when she knocked, but she knew he must be there, for the radio was playing; she could hear the sound of stringed instruments, scraping. After knocking a second time and still receiving no reply, she opened the door a crack and put her head around, and sure enough, there he was, sitting cross-legged in the middle of the floor, eyes closed, communing with the cat (and the stringed instruments).

"I've brought some heart," said Maggie. "And while

I'm here, have you got a screwdriver? I think the fuse has
blown on one of my plugs. I—"

"Sh!" Without opening his eyes, Sebastian reached up
a hand. Grasping her firmly by the arm, he pulled her
down onto the floor beside him.

"Look, I only want a screwdriver, I—"

"Quiet!" He clamped a hand over her mouth. "Listen
to the music."

Resigned, she propped herself against his shoulder,
legs stretched out in front, the ox heart in Dot's plastic
fridge pot balanced on her thighs.

Her thighs were still too fat. She hadn't kept to her
diet; after the first two weeks, it had gone by the board,
just as her diets always did. The sad truth was, she ate
too much—and talking of eating, she was ravenous right
now. It was hours since she had had lunch, and with Val
there to keep an eye on her she could never grab more
than a lousy salad and cottage cheese. She had to make
up for it in secret at night. Downstairs, waiting to be
cooked (when once Sebastian had returned to the land of
the living and lent her that screwdriver so that she could
mend the cooker plug), was a big juicy piece of steak,
which she had bought when she bought the cat's ox
heart. And here was she, stuck upstairs with her belly
rumbling, forced to sit through some rubbishing piece of
music that was all drones and groans and squeaking dis-
cord. She wasn't particularly musical at the best of times.
Especially not classical. She could recognize Beethoven's
Fifth and the *1812,* and that was about it. Heaven knew
what this thing was. How could he listen to it? It posi-
tively set one's teeth on edge. It didn't even have any
tune.

She said again: "Sebastian, I—"

"Tsh!"

"But I only w—"

"This is the last movement. Listen."

With a grimace, she subsided. At least a last movement was better than a first. If it had been the first, she would have screamed.

She could scream at this moment. How long did a last movement last for heaven's sake?

Self-control. Try listening. But *really* listening. After all, if Sebastian could get high on it, there must be something there. He might be crazy, but he wasn't an idiot.

She tried picking one instrument and following it through all its twistings and turnings. The sound wasn't so confusing when you did that. It began to make a kind of sense, acquire a sort of pattern. It was even, in its way, quite pleasant. Almost melodic. It did have a tune, under all the scrapings and groanings. You just had to take the trouble to listen for it.

"There," said Sebastian. "Wasn't that worth it?"

She wasn't prepared to go that far—not with her stomach rumbling and a piece of rump steak waiting to be cooked—but she conceded it hadn't been as bad as she had thought it was going to be. In fact, it had quite opened her eyes (or ears). She had always been firmly convinced that chamber music was nothing but cacophony.

"What was it?" she said.

"Quartet by Schubert. *Death and the Maiden.*"

Of course. It had to have death in it somewhere, didn't it? Sebastian was obsessed by death. *He* ought to have been a doctor, she thought. The first hundred corpses, and it might have cured him.

"Anyway," she said, "now that I'm allowed to talk

. . . do you have a screwdriver? I think the plug on my cooker has gone."

"I'll come look at it for you."

She was about to say he needn't bother, she could mend a fuse as well as the next person, when he opened the door of the bedside cupboard to rummage for a screwdriver, and the words turned into something else.

"Sebastian!" she said. "What on *earth*—"

He slammed the door guiltily. Maggie promptly opened it again. On the top shelf were no less than three full bottles of aspirin.

"Sebastian, are you—" She had been going to say "mad"; she bit it back. "What in heaven's name do you want with three bottles of aspirin?"

His eyes slid away. "You said it might be easier."

"Easier?"

"Than drowning oneself."

"For crying out loud!"

He was mad. He had to be. Whom did he think he was impressing?

"Sebastian, you can't be serious?"

"No." He pushed the lock of hair out of his eyes. "No, of course not."

"Then what have you got them for?"

"I—I don't know. I didn't know I had. You can have them if you want. Here." He swept up the bottles and thrust them at her. "You take them."

She hadn't the faintest idea what she was supposed to do with three bottles of aspirin—Pa had always strongly discouraged the taking of drugs in any shape or form—but she had the feeling it might be safer if she rather than Sebastian were to have custody of them. Not that he would ever actually put any of his veiled threats into practice, he was too busy posturing for that, but he could always do something stupid like spill them over the floor and leave them for the cat to get at.

Sunday accompanied them downstairs. She always went everywhere Sebastian went, and she liked Maggie's room because she could walk out onto the balcony, and from there onto next door's balcony, and thus right along to the end of the block. Sebastian opened up Maggie's plug and said the wires were bare and that whoever had put the plug on in the first place deserved to be shot. Fortunately it had not been Maggie. She could just as easily have set the matter to rights by herself, but she let Sebastian do it for her since he seemed to take it for granted that he should. In fact, she was always mildly amazed that he was capable of coping with ordinary domestic crises such as blown plugs and blocked sinks; he was such a thoroughly *ex*traordinary sort of person.

It was a pity he had to be so very extraordinary. There were times when he overdid it—like now. Having mended her plug and switched on the cooker, he turned his attention to the subject of her dinner. To her piece of rump steak. Lying there on its plate, doing no harm to anyone.

"You're not eating *that?*"

"Yes, I am," she said. She snatched at it defensively. "Why shouldn't I?"

"You know why you shouldn't! It's wicked, it's cruel— that was a live animal—a living, healthy creature. Look at it now! Just dead flesh on a plate! You ought to be ashamed."

"Well, I'm not. *I* didn't kill it." A specious argument. She knew it didn't stand up. But really Sebastian was enough to try the patience of a saint. "If it wasn't me, it would be someone else."

"But it is you—Maggie, don't! Don't eat it! I'm asking you . . . don't!"

"Look, it's *my* steak, *I* bought it—"

"Then let the cat have it!"

"*No!*"

As Sebastian made a lunge toward her, she jerked the plate out of his reach. The steak went flying; Sunday was on it in an instant.

"Leave her, leave her! Let her have it!"

Sebastian threw open the window. Sunday, the steak clamped between her jaws, needed no second invitation. Maggie flew after her but too late; she was already settled on next door's balcony, crouched over her prey, tearing at it with sharp teeth and deep, rumbling noises that were as much growl as purr.

"You idiot! You *idiot!*" Maggie turned back, panting, into the room. In that moment she could have murdered Sebastian. "You're mad!" she shrieked. "You know that? You're mad!"

"Maggie?" Sebastian stood, his hands hanging. It seemed suddenly to have struck him what he had done. "Maggie? I'm sorry, Maggie—" He took a step toward her, hesitant, apologetic. As well he might be. "Maggie, I'm sorry! I didn't mean it!"

"Bit late for that now."

"I'll get it back—I'll get it for you. It'll be all right. I'll get it."

Sebastian could do most things with Sunday, but one thing he couldn't do, and that was coax her into giving up a piece of rump steak once she had got it in her clutches. She knew too well what it was like to have gone short. Maggie watched in anguish as Sebastian swung himself over onto next door's balcony. For all she could have murdered him, she wouldn't want him falling to his death. A piece of rump steak wasn't worth that.

"Sebastian, leave it—"

The balconies had never been meant for walking on. They were there for decoration. Furthermore, the stonework was crumbling.

"Sebastian, *leave* it!" she said.

But he wouldn't. Sunday led him a dance over two more balconies before he finally managed to corner her.

"There! Told you I'd get it." Triumphantly he swung himself back over the sill. Sunday, with her fur all puffed up, came through like a cannonball behind him. "She hasn't eaten too much—it just needs a bit of a wash. Be as right as rain."

Maggie took the limp piece of flesh that he was holding out to her. One corner had disappeared, and all around the edge it was sodden and chewed. She looked at it, and she saw it through Sebastian's eyes. Her stomach heaved.

"What's the matter?" Sebastian sounded anxious. "It's not ruined. Most of it's still there. It'll cook up okay."

It probably would, but she just didn't fancy it anymore. She held it out between finger and thumb.

"Take—"

Sunday snatched and was gone. Sebastian looked at her uncertainly.

"But what are you going to eat?"

"Don't ask me," said Maggie. The cupboard wasn't exactly crammed with reserve stocks. One did one's shopping by the day; one didn't reckon on raving lunatics throwing one's dinner out of the window.

"It's all right!" Sebastian rushed to the door. "We'll make a curry."

Oh, would they? Sourly she said: "With what?"

"Anything—whatever we've got."

"Well, there's no curry powder for a start."

"I'll get some. Indian shop down the road."

"Yes, and it'll take *hours,* and I happen to be starving—*now.*"

"Wait there!"

She heard him galloping in his customary fashion, three at a time up the stairs, heard the door of his room crash open, and then shut. Within seconds he was back.

"Here!" He pushed a brown paper bag at her. "I'll go get the curry powder. You hang on. Shan't be two shakes of a duck's tail."

Sebastian disappeared. Maggie looked in the bag. It was full of little shriveled gray objects. Cautiously she tried one; it was quite tasty. She tried another, and then a whole handful, and before she knew it, she had guzzled half the bag.

It was only afterward, when she asked him, that he told her they were sunflower seeds. She never did tell Val.

9

The weeks passed. Sunday was neutered and grew sleek and complacent. Miss Everton, in shorthand, taught them "upward hay and downward chay" and marched the length of the board with her piece of chalk, chanting: "Hay-*chay!* Hay-*chay!* Hay-*chay!*" Maggie began a typing test with her fingers away from the home keys and continued as she had begun, with the result that after deductions for faults her speed came out as a minus. Miss Everton said she didn't know how anyone could be so stupid. She was always telling Maggie she was stupid. Val said it was because she didn't concentrate, and perhaps it was true. Try as she might, she couldn't manage to crawl inside that big black chimney she had told Sebastian about. Her mind kept flying off at tangents, and after half an hour of writing "hay-chay" in her shorthand notebook she felt like screaming.

"Technique is always boring," said Val. "It'll be different once you've mastered it."

If ever she did—but then she must. It was a means to an end, and anyhow, it wasn't clever to be stupid. Not at *any*thing.

Sometimes, in the week, Sebastian would come down

to her room and they would make a vegetable curry to-gether—or Sebastian would make a vegetable curry and Maggie would sit chewing sunflower seeds until it was ready. Sebastian was quite good at concocting vegetarian messes. He could work wonders with a few beans and lentils and fortunately had no objection to eggs, though when one evening she tentatively suggested fish, on the ground of fish being cold-blooded and therefore, pre-sumably, not having feelings, he asked her sternly how she knew they hadn't.

"Just because they're not soft and cuddly . . . they're still living creatures, aren't they?"

"Yes, I suppose so," said Maggie with a sigh.

"Could *you* catch one? Could *you* watch it fighting for breath and feel happy about it?"

"No, I suppose not," said Maggie, and she gave an-other sigh. And then she perked up and said: "What about things like prawns?"

"What about them?" said Sebastian. "The principle is the same."

There wasn't really any argument. Occasionally, guilt-ily, she would smuggle herself in some sausages or a few slices of ham, and now and again at Chislehurst she would have a blowout on one of Dot's roasts. But then, damn and blast Sebastian, she would suddenly find her-self thinking, halfway through the meal, *This was a living creature that you're eating; this was a healthy, happy, innocent ani-mal,* and she would start having visions of little fluffy lambs and squeaking pink piglets, and the meat would begin to taste bloody and fleshly, and she would have to force herself to swallow it.

One Sunday, after Dot had had her baby, she took Sebastian down there with her. She had warned him there would be meat and that he wasn't to start lecturing about it. He had promised that he wouldn't, and he didn't; instead, he fled from the table with a hand pressed to his mouth, which was almost as bad, if not worse. It was one of those moments when she found herself in agreement with Jimmy: Sebastian was a *pain*. Happily he redeemed himself afterward by mooning over the baby, which made Dot's day because in spite of having done her stint in obstetrics, which one would have thought was enough to cure anybody, she had still managed to go all starry-eyed and goo-gooish. For her part, Maggie wasn't too wild about tiny babies. Sebastian, on the other hand, was enraptured. He crooned enough to satisfy even Dot. As they were preparing to leave, Dot touched Maggie's hand and said: "That's a nice boy. You ought to stick with him."

Somehow—she was never quite sure how—she allowed herself to be bludgeoned not only into eating sunflower seeds and vegetable curry but also into helping him sell his newspapers in the square. Val could hardly believe it.

"Honestly," she said. "You're getting as cracked as he is."

Maybe she was, if cracked was what it was called. Was it cracked to care about things? Or was it only cracked if you cared enough to get up and start shouting? She knew she could never commit herself with the same degree of passion as Sebastian. A short while ago he had given her a heap of stickers saying "SAVE THE WHALE" and "STOP SEAL SLAUGHTER" and had told her to "plaster them on places," but after furtively slapping one onto a butcher's shopwindow and another onto a lamppost on her way home late from Val's one night, and being convinced that half the street was spying on her from behind the curtains, she became self-conscious and hid the rest in her desk at college, where they reproached her every time she opened the lid.

Sebastian, with the fervor of the true fanatic, stuck posters everywhere, even in broad daylight. There were occasions, it had to be admitted (such as when he absented himself from Dot's dinner table or threw pieces of rump steak to the cat), when Sebastian's obsessions could be tiresome; there were other occasions, such as when he harangued people in the street, when they could be a decided embarrassment. Yet, for all that, you had to respect him. At least he cared; it was more than most people did.

They had taken recently, when Maggie was not going to Chislehurst, as she was tending to do less and less, to going off on long tramps together in the country. They would catch the bus at the top of Station Road and get off six stops later at Coney Halt, where, provided you knew the footpaths, as Sebastian did inside out, you could walk for miles at a time without ever having to set foot upon a road. Val grumbled that Maggie was becoming "all horrid and hike-ish" and only shuddered when Maggie suggested that she and Shalid might join them.

"We've got better things to do on a Sunday morning than go traipsing through fields full of mud—especially with that loony. I don't know what you see in him."

Val wouldn't, of course. Maggie didn't bother to try explaining; she knew it would only be a waste of breath.

One evening, moved by a rare burst of conscience, she was actually practicing some shorthand in her shorthand notebook when there was a crashing at the door and Sebastian appeared.

"What d'you want?" She spoke without looking up, absorbed in her task of perfecting circle s's.

"*I,*" said Sebastian, "have got *bicycles.*"

"Really?" Circle s, circle s, circle s. "Try ignoring them, maybe they'll go away." Or maybe he would.

"But I have got *two* bicycles . . . one bicycle for you, one bicycle for me."

With a sigh Maggie abandoned her circle s's and permitted herself a quick glance. Sebastian was standing in the doorway, beaming at her, Sunday perched on his shoulder like Long John Silver's parrot.

"Two," he said. He held up two fingers. "And both in working order."

She wrinkled her forehead. "How?"

"How?"

"How have you got two?" A week ago he hadn't even had one. They had discussed the possibility of buying, until they had seen the prices.

"Found 'em," said Sebastian. "In the old shed at the bottom of the garden."

"But the shed's kept locked."

"I know. I forced the window. I was down there looking for Sunday."

He was down there looking for Sunday, and all of a sudden he thought he would force the window. Maggie shook her head.

"It's okay," said Sebastian. "It's not vandalism. No one's been in there for about a century."

"In that case I shouldn't have thought the machines were going to be much use."

"The machines are fine. Come have a look."

She hesitated. She really *was* meant to be doing circle s's. They were having a speed test tomorrow.

"It's dark," she said.

"Not so dark you can't see. . . . Come on!"

Oh, well. The circle *s*'s could always wait for later. She'd better go gaze on his wretched bicycles before he took it into his head to start breaking into something else.

He had been quite right about the shed: Human foot had not trod its mildewed boards for many a long year. Probably not since the house had been turned into apartments, and heaven only knew when that had been. But if Sebastian was right about the shed, Maggie reckoned she was going to be proved right about the bicycles. She had never seen anything like them. They looked as if they were made of cast iron. One had the remnants of a wicker basket attached to the handlebars; the other had a saddlebag which disintegrated even as she touched it.

"They're quite solid," said Sebastian.

"Oh, they're solid," said Maggie.

"They only need an overhaul. Tires pumped up, brake blocks checked . . . nothing to it."

"But they're not ours," said Maggie.

"Not ours, not anyone's."

No, and in any case, property was theft, wasn't it? And furthermore, if people were selfish enough to leave perfectly good bicycles lying around to rot in damp garden sheds when they could have been given to someone who would have appreciated them, then they deserved to have them appropriated.

"Okay," said Maggie. "So where d'you want to go?"

"Ever been to Knole?"

"No. What's Knole?"

"Knole Park."

"Don't know it."

"Don't know Knole Park? Ye gods! The ignorance!"

"All right, so I'm ignorant. Where is it?"

"Knole Park, lady, is but a few short miles hence . . . Sevenoaks, to be precise. We could cycle it easily."

"When?"

"Next Saturday?"

"All right. If you really want."

"You'll like it there. I promise."

"Why? What's to see?"

"Well, there's a house—and there's a park. National Trust. I don't imagine the house is likely to be open, not at this time of year, but the park will be. The park's always open. They've got a couple of herds of tame deer in there."

"I see! You want to go talk to the deer!"

He grinned, unabashed. "Why not? I like deer."

"Oh, you'd like hippopotamuses if you could cuddle them."

"Probably," said Sebastian.

10

It was pleasant at Knole, she had to agree; it was worth the cycle ride. She couldn't imagine why the family had never come here for days out, seeing as it was within such easy reach, but looking back, she realized that the family, as a family, never had gone for days out together. Ma and Pa were not really "days out" sort of people. It had been all book learning and catching up on world affairs for them. No wonder she was so abysmally ignorant when it came to the countryside and wildlife.

Knole House itself, as Sebastian had predicted, was closed to visitors, though even if it hadn't been, neither of them was in sufficient funds to have paid the entrance fee. Sebastian's job on the building site had come to an end, and he was what he described as "skint," which she took to mean penniless. She herself was in not much better case. She had barely enough in her bank account to cover the rest of the term's rent. Doubtless if she had applied to Pa, although he would have grumbled, he would have helped out, but it would have been too great an admission of failure. Sebastian didn't go running to Mommy and Daddy the minute he found himself in difficulties; neither would she.

Since they couldn't go into the house, they contented themselves with walking around the perimeter, at the foot of the high brick wall which guarded it, and at intervals peering in through the wrought iron gates at the gardens beyond.

"I feel like the poor-children-who-couldn't-go-to-the-party," said Maggie.

"We are," said Sebastian. "Nobody invited us."

The acres of parkland seemed totally deserted, for they saw not a soul save the deer, which followed at their heels in quest of food, frisking after them from all directions, with bulky bodies precariously aloft on spindly legs, up the hillside. At the top of a rise, with the house spread out below them, all turrets and pinnacles like a medieval town, they unpacked a lunch of cheese rolls and hard-boiled eggs, apples, bananas, and the inevitable sunflower seeds. It seemed that deer were partial to almost everything, even including hard-boiled eggs. Fortunately Maggie had had the foresight to make allowances (for herself and the deer. She tended to discount Sebastian where catering arrangements were concerned. He had an appetite like a sparrow).

In spite of its being December, the weather was mild and almost springlike. Maggie lay back, contented, propped on her elbows, watching Sebastian make friends with a particularly nervous doe, which had to be coaxed. Sebastian was in one of his blessedly normal moods, when not even Chris could have claimed there was anything odd about him. (Unless you counted talking to deer as odd, as Chris, being Chris, probably would.) She watched the doe take a tentative step closer; then another, a bit closer; then another, and finally another, until at last the doe was pushing at Sebastian's hand for the food that she knew was to be found there. She watched Sebastian stroke the soft muzzle with its twitching nostrils and rub his cheek against the dappled fur. Why couldn't he always be like this? she wondered. Nice and normal, without any complexes. What could be more idyllic than the two of them, up here, on the hillside, miles from the stench of civilization, nothing but themselves and the deer and the occasional rustle of some small creature in the grass?

Sebastian, as if catching her thoughts, said: "What is so fantastic is that they can keep the place open all year round and nobody ever comes in and wreaks havoc."

Unlike the local gardens, where saplings were regularly uprooted and benches hacked to pieces and even the ducks on the pond found massacred.

Sebastian, as if still catching her thoughts, said: "They're so bloody trusting." He blew gently up the doe's nostrils. The doe twitched her scraggy fly whisk of a tail in appreciation. "They'd go to anyone that offered them a handful of food. Think how easy it would be for some pervert to run amok with a knife."

Maggie frowned. She didn't want to think about perverts running amok with knives. It was too lovely a day for that sort of thing.

"Imagine coming in one morning and finding them all with their throats cut or their eyes put out . . . it's what people do. It's what they do to animals. There was a dog near us. Old Labrador. Used to go to the gate and talk to people. Know what they did? They set fire to her. Threw fuel over her and—"

"Sebastian!" She screamed it at him, shooting herself upright with such force that the doe, taking fright, went galloping off down the hillside. "Will you stop that?"

Why, oh, why! Why did he always have to go ruin everything? A heavenly day like this, and he had to start telling her about people setting fire to old Labradors.

"What's *wrong* with you?" she said. "Why do you have to *do* it all the time?"

He was staring at her, hurt and bewildered. "Do what?"

"Talk about death—all the *time*—always *on* about it."

"But she didn't die. She—"

"Will you shut up? Will you just *shut up?* I don't want to hear!"

She flung herself down again. For a time there was silence. Maggie lay on her back, staring up at the sky, her heart still pounding with rage against Sebastian. She strove for calming thoughts, trying to recapture the shattered idyll of a moment ago. What Sebastian was doing, she didn't know. Nor did she particularly care. He was an idiot. She wasn't surprised people got sick of him; she was pretty sick of him herself.

Gradually the calming thoughts took over. As always, her rage subsided. However much you might want to, it simply wasn't possible to remain mad at Sebastian for very long. He so plainly never intended to upset or annoy. All very well for Chris and Mick and the rest of them to say he did it only to gain attention; Maggie wasn't so sure. And besides, for someone to need attention as badly as all that—

She rolled over onto her side. Sebastian, with an air of deep concentration, was shredding a blade of grass. Suddenly she felt like a louse.

"I'm sorry," she said.

"Sorry?"

"For yelling at you."

" 'S all right."

"It's just—"

"I know. I get on your nerves."

"It's not that. But why do you always have to think of horrid things?"

Sebastian demolished his blade of grass and looked around for another. "I don't always."

"You do pretty often."

He bent his head. "Don't you?"

"Not if I can help it."

"Not ever?"

"Well—occasionally, I suppose." Occasionally dark thoughts crossed everyone's mind. "But I don't wallow in them."

"I don't wallow in them. When you say 'wallow,' that implies enjoyment."

"So if you don't enjoy it—"

"I can't help it. It's something that just happens." With extreme care, he began dividing a second blade of grass, exactly down the center. "I don't want to think horrid things. I'm not a masochist. I don't get any kick out of—" He stopped.

"Out of what?" said Maggie.

Sebastian ruined his second blade of grass and leaned forward for another.

"Out of what?" said Maggie.

He ruined another two blades before he replied, and then it was obliquely. "Sometimes," he said, "I find myself looking at Sunday, and suddenly—"

Again he stopped.

"Suddenly?" said Maggie.

"Suddenly, I—I see her—c-cut open, or—or d-dismembered, or—or in p-pain and s-screaming, and I"—he pushed at his hair—"I get scared in case—case it means that—s-subconsciously it's what I r-really w-want—"

Up there, on the hillside, miles from civilization, Maggie felt a chill creep through her. *You weren't at school with the bloke. . . . You don't know what a nut he is.*

"I don't l-*like* thinking things like that," said Sebastian. Maggie swallowed.

"But don't you ever?" He turned to her, appealing. "Don't you have v-visions of things? Th-things you'd rather not?"

He was regarding her earnestly. He wanted her to say something; he wanted reassurance. Maggie shook herself. Sebastian might be all mixed up, but he wasn't capable of harming a fly. No matter what grotesque thoughts he might have. She sat up.

"No, I can't say that I do," she said. "Not in that way. But I think that's probably because I haven't any imagination. I told you . . . I was science, not languages. I think people with imagination tend to let it run away with them. But it's stupid to let yourself think that *you* could do anything to Sunday. I mean, I can understand being scared some vivisectionist might get hold of her, or louts off the street. Something like that. The trouble is you go and dwell on it; you let it get all out of proportion. That's when you start getting morbid. The thing to do is think of other things. *Don't* think of Sunday being cut open. Just don't let yourself. Start thinking of something beautiful, instead. Like a poem, or a piece of music, or—"

"I've tried," said Sebastian. "I can't."

"Of course you can! It's just a question of control. *Saying* to yourself, 'I am not going to think about this thing. I'm going to think about a poem.' And then by the time you've thought about the poem, you've forgotten about the other."

Sebastian turned back to his blade of grass.

"I had this rabbit once," he said.

Maggie looked at him warily. "Oh?"

"It was when I was little. Well—quite little. His name was Clarence. He lived in a hutch in the yard. I used to take him out and play with him. He was like a dog; he'd follow you."

Maggie found that her throat had gone dry.

"And what—what happened to him?"

"I used to torture myself in bed at night, seeing him lying down there with his throat cut . . . thinking it might be me that was going to do it to him."

Maggie moistened her lips with the tip of her tongue. "And—did you?"

"Did I?" Sebastian looked around at her vaguely. "No. No, of course I didn't. How could I? I loved him."

"So what happened?"

"Nothing happened. He died of old age."

Maggie relaxed. "I thought you were going to tell me something horrid! What was the point of all that?"

"Oh—" Sebastian shrugged. "I don't know. Perhaps there wasn't one."

He certainly was a very strange sort of boy. There could be no denying it. But still he wasn't the pain that they all said.

"Tell me." Maggie shuffled herself farther forward, so that she was on a level with him. "Where do your parents live? I know they're local, but—"

Sebastian plucked another blade of grass. "Out Farley Oaks way."

"Farley Oaks Farm? Is that theirs?"

He grunted, presumably to signify that it was.

"Don't you ever go see them?"

"Hardly ever."

"Wouldn't they like you to?"

"Shouldn't think so. Why should they?"

"Well—I don't know. Parents usually do." Even Ma and Pa wouldn't like it if she stayed away for good, and they were hardly what you would call doting. "Surely your mother would like to see you?" she said.

Sebastian, in search of more grass, found a pebble and flung it. He didn't say anything.

"Don't you get on?" said Maggie. "I don't terribly with mine. At least—sometimes I do. Other times I don't. It's my mother mostly. But I suppose one still loves them." She considered it awhile. "They are one's parents after all. One doesn't have any others." She looked at Sebastian. "Do you love yours?"

He hunched a shoulder.

"S'pose I might have loved my mother."

"Might have done?" She was alarmed. "She's not dead, is she?"

"Nope."

"You mean, she's—gone away or something?"

"Nope."

Plainly he was not going to volunteer any information. Maggie thought perhaps it might be wiser to drop the subject of his mother.

"How about your father?" she said. "Don't you love him?" In her experience, fathers were more lovable than mothers, but perhaps that was only because she was a girl. The old sex thing rearing its ugly head.

Sebastian flung a second pebble, rather vigorously.

"You can't love people who kill things. Kill things and then eat them. Then try to force you to."

"They're always trying to force you into things," said Maggie. "Mine tried to force me into going to medical school. Did you have rows?"

"I just used to get sick. I used to bring it all up. Then he didn't try it anymore; he didn't talk to me; he said I was a driveling idiot and ought to be put away."

"Your father?" Maggie was shocked. Pa had on several occasions informed her that she was a blasted nincompoop or a hen-brained half-wit, but somehow that was different. To tell someone he ought to be put away . . . "Your *father* said it?" she said.

"He said I needed looking at. It was very vexatious for him . . . killing all those things and me not eating them. We fought each other once. I tried to stop him from shooting rabbits. He said he had a good mind to blow my head off."

Maggie opened her eyes in astonishment. "Sounds to me as if he's the one that needed looking at."

"He's a very violent man. You have to be, to kill things."

She watched while he flung three more pebbles down the hill. She was trying to get the picture of how it must have been, Sebastian having meat forced upon him and promptly being sick and his father saying he was a driveling idiot and ought to be put away.

"What did your mother say? Didn't she ever stick up for you?"

"My mother? My mother rides to hounds."

It wasn't exactly an answer, yet at the same time it was. She began to see that the bosom of his family was not the ideal setting for Sebastian.

"So what will you do at Christmas?" she said.

"Won't do anything at Christmas. Stay in Station Road."

"But won't you be lonely?"

"No more than usual."

Maggie remembered what Mick had said about Sebastian's being a loner: "Always has been."

"It's not good to be lonely at Christmas," she said. The house would be almost empty. Mick and Paula were going off to Paula's mother; the Spanish housekeeper was going to Spain; the Graces were bound to take themselves off somewhere. That would leave only Peter and Jimmy, and she couldn't see them inviting Sebastian down. Peter might, but not Jimmy. Jimmy could be as piglike as Chris. "Tell you what," she said, "why not come up to Birmingham with me?"

"What, for Christmas?"

"Well, that's what we were talking about."

Sebastian looked at her very solemnly. "Are you sure?"

Actually, of course, the minute she'd said it she'd begun to get cold feet—what on earth was Chris going to say? And Ma, if he ran away from the table? And Pa, if he started spouting socialism?—but it was too late to retract now.

"Course I'm sure! How could I sit up there stuffing mince pies and Christmas pudding and"—she almost said roast turkey—"and nuts, and sweets, and things, knowing that you're going to be stuck down here with a packet of lousy sunflower seeds? Anyway, you'd be moral support." What she meant by that, she had no idea, except that it sounded good. "Do come," she said. "Please! It'll make me ever so much happier. And you can't *really* want to stay down here by yourself. You'll only be prey to morbid thoughts. Especially at this time of year. Come up to Birmingham and see if my awful parents are any less awful than yours."

Timidly he said: "But won't I annoy them? I seem to annoy most people."

She was about to tell him that if he would only make a determined effort and act normally for once, then there wouldn't be any problem, but she changed her mind and said instead: "You don't annoy me."

"Yes, I do; you shout at me."

"Oh! Well! If I can't do *that* from time to time—"

"And what about your brother? He thinks I'm a pain."

"Yes, and I think *he's* a pain. . . . You don't have to worry about Chris. It's my home just as much as it is his. If I want to invite someone, then I can invite someone. And this year I happen to have invited *you,* and that's all there is to it, so Chris can just get lost."

On the way home Maggie's bicycle developed a puncture. They stopped and pumped it up, but it was flat again within seconds. Needless to say, they had no puncture repair outfit, and even if they had, according to Sebastian, it wouldn't have done them any good.

"I didn't like to tell you before, but I'm surprised we've managed to make it this far; the whole of the inner tube has gone."

"What do you mean, the whole of the inner tube has gone?"

"I mean it's finished. Perished. Had it."

"My inner tube? *Perished?* You've let me go cycling around on a *perished inner tube? Knowing* that sooner or later it was going to give up?"

"Well . . . I thought it was worth a gamble. Seeing as we could neither of us afford to splash out on a new one."

"I see!" Maggie breathed very deeply. "So what, pray, are we supposed to do now?"

"Guess we'll have to hoof it," said Sebastian. He said it with maddening cheerfulness. "It's only a few miles."

"Only a few miles!" She glared at him. "It would serve you right if I took yours and left you to get back by yourself."

"Can if you like."

"I've a good mind to."

"Well, go on, then. I don't mind."

"Oh!" Infuriated, she thumped with clenched fist on her saddle. "There are times when you absolutely annoy me!"

11

It was fortunate, since by Christmas they were down to literally their last meter coin and had been reduced to sharing a baked potato for dinner and huddling beneath blankets of an evening to keep warm, that Dot and Francis were also going up to Birmingham (to show off the new arrival) and had offered them a lift. It had been that or hitching—or else breaking open the gas meters and buying new inner tubes for Maggie's bike. Sebastian's idea, needless to say.

"You must be joking," said Maggie. "I'm not cycling all the way up there on that rattletrap."

"Do you good," said Sebastian. "You know you're always going on about losing weight."

"Yes, well, I'd rather not lose it that way, thank you very much. . . . Anyhow, what happens when they come to empty the meters?"

Sebastian tapped the side of his nose and said he had ways of getting into gas meters so that nobody knew they had been opened, and since the landlord was charging at least twice as much per unit as he ought, it would only be taking back what they shouldn't have had to put in in the first place. They were still arguing about the ethics of it when Dot rang up and solved the problem.

"Yes, *please,*" said Maggie. "We should love to."

"We shan't be leaving till Christmas Eve. About lunch-time. Is that all right? Or were you planning on going before? . . . You what? . . . Oh, Maggie! You haven't? Why on earth didn't you say? I'll send you something immediately. . . . Yes, I will, I insist! You can't go on living on baked potatoes for the rest of the week. I knew this would happen. It's not as easy as you think, trying to budget over a three-month period. Especially when you're not used to it. I do wish you'd told me."

The following morning a check for five pounds dropped on the mat. There were definitely advantages, thought Maggie, to having a sister like Dot. She might be a bit of an old mother hen, but you could always rely on her. She took the check out and flashed it triumphantly at Sebastian.

"What shall we do with it? Be sensible and make it last? Or blow it all"—visions of fish and chips, sausages and mash, steak and kidney pudding; she looked at him, eagerly—"blow it all," she said, "on one mad binge?"

"You're not going to spend it on your*self?*" said Sebastian. "What about Sunday?"

"Oh—" She had forgotten about Sunday. She supposed it wasn't quite fair expecting a cat to exist indefinitely on a diet of baked potato and scraps filched from other people's dinner plates. She sighed; the vision of fish and chips receded whence it had come, out of the land of dreams. Sebastian wouldn't have allowed it in any case.

"Whatever happens," he said, "we've got to make sure that Sunday's all right."

He at least let her buy some butter to go with the baked potatoes. It was his sole concession.

On Christmas Eve, while waiting for Dot and Francis to arrive, they exchanged presents. They had made a pact, back in the days of relative affluence, when they could still afford sunflower seeds and vegetable curry, that they would buy each other "something small and useful and insignificant in price." Maggie, accordingly, had bought Sebastian a bumper pack of razor blades because he always claimed never to have any; Sebastian, from whom she had confidently been expecting bubble bath or talcum powder, had bought her a pair of frilly panties because "you did say something small and useful."

"Don't know how *useful* they're going to be," said Maggie, but she said it only to cover up a sudden bashfulness. No one had ever given her frilly panties before. She wasn't that sort of girl. It was different for Val. People were always giving her little frivolous bits of this and that, but not stolid, commonsensical Maggie. Maggie-with-the-brains and the three A-levels. A facecloth or a padded coathanger was what she normally got. She felt a tinge of pinkness creep into her cheeks.

"Are you blushing?" said Sebastian.

"Me?" said Maggie. "I don't blush." And it was true; as a rule, she did not. "Anyway," she said, *"yours* is useful. At least you won't be able to make excuses anymore. Just as well—Pa goes absolutely berserk if people are scruffy. Chris came home with a beard last year, and he made him take it off. He said he wasn't having the filthy thing in the house. They almost came to blows. It's one of his things—like socialism. That's another. Gets him really hot under the collar. Anyone says 'socialism,' and his eyes go all bloodshot . . . I just thought I ought to warn you."

"It's all right," said Sebastian. "I won't breathe a word."

"And you—you won't go on about vegetarianism, will you?" Vegetarianism was what the parents called cranky. It was as cranky as being a Plymouth Brother or a Jehovah's Witness or indeed anything at all with which they happened not to agree. "Just tell them that you don't like meat. Tell them you don't like the taste of it, or you're allergic to it or something." They would understand that. It wasn't necessarily cranky to be allergic. There were actually people in the world who couldn't help it if they burst into rashes and spots; it was something to do with their blood chemistry. Even Pa didn't expect people to be able to control their own blood chemistry. "You could say it's something," she said, "to do with animal protein." She looked at him. "Just for once," she said. "Couldn't you?"

"If that's what you want."

"I know it's against all your principles, but—"

There was a pause.

"It's not as if you'd stand any chance of converting them."

Another pause.

"You'd only get into an argument, and then Pa would start shouting, and—"

"Do you think it might be better," said Sebastian, "if I didn't come?"

"No!" She was horrified. (Guilty, too, because it was exactly what she had been thinking.) "Of course, you're coming. I've asked you, haven't I?"

"You could always unask me. I'd understand." He

turned the box of razor blades between his fingers. "I know most people think I'm a pain."

Maggie frowned. She looked at him as he stood there, head bent, the familiar lock of hair falling into his eyes. Sebastian for once had made an effort. He had borrowed an iron from the housekeeper and pressed his trousers, and some darning wool from Sandy Grace, with which he had cobbled together the elbows of his sweater. He had polished up his boots and washed his hair and even scraped his chin with a blunt razor blade—and all in honor of Maggie's parents. Stoutly she said: *"I* don't think you're a pain."

"Don't you?" said Sebastian.

"No," said Maggie, "I don't."

Sebastian raised his head. There was a hint of laughter in his eyes. "Oh, Maggie, what a liar!" he said.

She was glad, at that moment, that the doorbell rang. "Come on! There's Dot and Francis. Grab your stuff."

"You mean you're really willing to run the risk?"

She tossed her head. "You're the one that's running all the risk. . . . If you do anything to disgrace me, I shall clobber you."

"I wish we could take Sunday."

"Well, we can't; you know we can't. Bess would go crazy. Anyhow, it's only three days, and Peter's promised faithfully he'll come up and feed her. She'll be perfectly all right. She can look out of the window and curl up on the bed and—oh, come *on,* Sebastian! She's only a cat."

Dot and Francis were waiting for them in the car. The car was six years old and built like a battleship, as safe and staid and comfortable as Francis himself, but even so, now that she had the baby, Dot wouldn't sit in the front. She had a theory the back was safer, having a trunkful of luggage behind it to absorb all the blows. (Not to mention a fuel tank.) She said: "I hope you didn't want to sit and hold hands because if you did, I'm afraid one of you will have to sit back to front." How quaint and Dot-like! To think that she and Sebastian might want to hold hands. Surely anyone could see they didn't have that sort of relationship? Anyone but Dot. Dot, no doubt, would find it rather touching and romantic if they were at the silly, sick-making stage of spooning and mooning. Maggie had never spooned and mooned with anyone and certainly couldn't imagine doing so with Sebastian. Still, there was one thing to be said in Dot's favor: *She* obviously didn't think he was a pain.

They drove up to Birmingham with Maggie in the front, where she could keep an eye on the road signs and do any necessary map reading (she prided herself on her map reading; Dot was quite hopeless), and Sebastian in the back, where, if he wanted, he could hold hands with the baby. Maggie was only too glad not to have to sit next to it. It might *look* all pink and clean, but it smelled distinctly of sick. It was her experience that babies always did.

They didn't reach Birmingham until almost dinnertime, having gone completely haywire coming off the motorway, in spite of Maggie's map reading and detailed instructions from Pa. The parents had installed themselves in the nice middle-class suburb of Edgbaston, in a nice middle-class house, Victorian and double-fronted, which somewhat surprisingly had Sebastian in ecstasies. (It turned out he actually *liked* Victoriana. There was never any telling with Sebastian.) Jesse was there, and Chris as well. She had been half hoping Chris might have gone off with friends, but no such luck. Jesse took one look at Sebastian and said: "Hello! Don't I remember you from Trinity?"

Chris said: "Yes. He was a snot-nosed brat along with me when you were lording it over us."

"That's right," said Jesse. "I seem to remember telling you not to swing on the hot-water pipes."

"And then he promptly swung on them."

"Didn't you all?" said Jesse dryly.

Apart from the occasional agonized signaling across the room when Sebastian's back was turned and the occasional abortive attempt to get her alone and ask her what in heaven's name she thought she was playing at, Chris conducted himself reasonably well. At any rate there weren't any gibes or snide remarks. Sebastian conducted himself more than just reasonably well; for the whole of that first evening he behaved with such exemplary normality that she almost wondered whether he was feeling all right. He even managed to endure the sight of veal escalopes at the dinner table. It was Maggie who did all the flinching. She had never been too happy about veal, even back in the good old days before vegetable curries and sunflower seeds had begun to rule her life. Even then she had felt a twinge. Now, thanks to Sebastian, she felt positive guilt. Veal calves were an obscenity. They were as bad as factory hens, or beagles in laboratories, or—

Her eye, vainly attempting to escape, encountered Sebastian's across the table. He looked at her steadily but said nothing. Neither, to her shame, did she. Simply pushed her plate away with the muttered excuse that she had eaten two bars of chocolate in the car and wasn't hungry. Since, in fact, she was ravenous, she supposed it could be taken as some sort of gesture, but it didn't exactly make her proud of herself.

She wasn't very surprised when Sebastian, next morning, cornered her rather desperately with the demand to be told what he was to do.

"I'm scared I shall say something, and then you'll get mad at me. But just sitting there, watching—it's like watching someone flog a horse to death and not lifting a finger to stop it. You can't just say *nothing*. Not if you believe in something."

This time yesterday Maggie might have told him not to be so melodramatic; after the way the family had dug into those veal escalopes she was more inclined to sympathize. How could anyone bring themselves, with clear consciences, to eat veal? How could they do it without being tortured at every mouthful by thoughts of those pathetic, helpless, anemic calves, shut away from the sunlight and forced to lick their own urine? It was barbarous; it was inhuman. Sebastian was quite right: One ought not to sit there and say nothing.

"We'll tell them the truth," she said. "We'll tell them straight out that you can't stand the sight of people devouring flesh." What did it matter if they thought he was cranky? They would probably have thought William Wilberforce was, trying to stop the slave trade.

Ma raised both eyebrows into her hairline when Maggie explained that Sebastian would like to stay away from the table until the meat course was over.

"He's not being rude. It's just that he feels the same way about people eating animals as you do about abortions."

"Oh! Well! I suppose everyone's entitled to his own point of view," said Ma, who, in fact, thought that some people shouldn't be allowed any point of view at all. "Personally"—she gave one of her small, sarcastic trills— "I should scarcely have thought that the humane slaughter of animals came into quite the same category as the murder of unborn children, but there you are. It's a free country. Universal franchise. If he prefers to set animals above human beings, who am I to argue?"

Sebastian's absence from the dinner table, just as she had known that it would, provoked Chris into one of his displays of derision. "Wondered how long it would be before he had a breakout . . . what's the trouble? Can't face dead turkey?"

Pa looked at Maggie in some irritation. "You haven't gone and foisted some crank vegetarian on us?"

"He may be a crank," said Dot, "but he's marvelous with the baby."

"Course he is," said Chris. "Probably wishes he could have one of his own. Anyone who goes to bed with three teddy bears—"

"He does not!"

Maggie slammed down her fork. Jesse regarded her thoughtfully. Chris, leaning forward, said: "Oh! And how do *you* know what he goes to bed with?"

"I know because I know. Because he hasn't *got* a teddy bear. He was just putting you on, and like an idiot, you fell for it."

Chris scowled. He didn't like being called an idiot.

"What are you doing with the bloke anyway?"

"Just being normally friendly," said Maggie.

"Normally friendly! No one can be normally anything with a nut like that."

At the back of her eyes Maggie felt an ominous pricking sensation like tears. *(Tears? Her?)* She blinked angrily.

"There are times, Chris Easter, when you are so un*char*-itable—"

"Well, why did you have to go bring him here? You know perfectly well what I think about him."

"Yes, and so does he!" A tear spurted out and landed with a splash on the end of her nose. She brushed it away, furious. *"He* knows you think he's a pain. You never take any trouble to conceal it, do you? Never care about anyone else's feelings. Only *yours.* Always *yours."*

"Don't tell me you've gone and *fallen* for him?" said Chris. "Not *Sebastian?"*

"Why shouldn't she?" said Dot. "He happens to be an extremely nice boy."

"Yeah? Well, for your information he also happens to be as mad as a flaming hatter."

"Don't say that!" Maggie had pushed back her chair and was on her feet. "I've told you before . . . just *don't say it!"*

"I'll say what I want to say! You don't tell me what to say and what not!"

Pa gave a groan. "They're off."

Rows between Chris and Maggie were commonplace enough. They had been having slanging matches ever since they were old enough to kick each other under the table and call each other pig and cat and lousy, stinking liar. As a rule, Maggie could more than hold her own. Today she was hampered by a weakness to which she almost never succumbed, and certainly not in public— certainly not in front of *Chris.* What, for heaven's sake, was the matter with her? It wasn't as if he were saying anything he hadn't said before. She dashed the back of her hand across her eyes. Small wonder Jesse was puckering his brow and Dot looking concerned. How she did *despise* females who wept.

"Mag—"

Jesse plucked at her elbow, trying to make her sit down again. She shook him off impatiently: impatient with herself rather than with Jesse.

"He oughtn't to say things like that. He ought to be more careful about the words he chooses. He doesn't go around calling people niggers or queers, so why does he go around calling them mad?"

"Because some of them are flaming mad! Some of them are flaming loopy!"

She had never actually thrown anything at anyone before, not even at Chris. It gave a great deal of momentary satisfaction. Ma said later: "I don't blame you—not at all. It does one good to let off steam occasionally. I just wish you hadn't chosen the salt. It did make such a mess." At the time she didn't stay long enough to see the results of her handiwork. She turned and fled before she could disgrace herself utterly.

She fled down the long Victorian passage to the womblike warmth of the kitchen. She had forgotten Sebastian was out there; she caught him picking bits off the turkey for Bess. He straightened up guiltily.

"I was just—" And then, at the sight of her face: "Maggie? What's wrong?"

She shook her head; the tears, like a fountain, went spurting out over her cheeks. Sebastian pushed the turkey carcass to one side. Awkwardly he put his arms around her.

"Don't cry, Maggie . . . I don't like to see you cry."

No, it was too out of character, wasn't it? Maggie was strong; Maggie was sensible; Maggie didn't cry.

Except that on this occasion she did. Woefully and shamefully, with her head buried in Sebastian's shoulder and her tears making a damp patch—nay, a sodden, soaking wet patch—on his newly darned sweater, and Bess sitting on her haunches, howling for the turkey.

And then, quite suddenly, instead of weeping over him, she found that she was kissing him—or he was kissing her, or they were kissing each other. It took her by surprise, for she had never thought of Sebastian in that way, but once she had got over the initial amazement, it seemed the most natural thing in the world to be kissing Sebastian in the kitchen on Christmas Day while the rest of them sat in the dining room, eating slaughtered turkey.

And suddenly, as well, she saw him in a different light. He wasn't just long, lanky Sebastian, whom she took for granted, but really quite beautiful Sebastian, whom she had never properly looked at before. Not the gauche youth who maddened her by his follies and ineptitudes, but a fully fledged member of the opposite sex. And she, too—surely she was different? Surely she couldn't still be the same solid, stolid, unimaginative Maggie that she had been? At any rate she knew now what Val got out of wrapping herself around Shalid's neck at parties or standing with him for hours, immobile, under lampposts. It had always been something of a mystery—and it had taken Sebastian to solve it for her.

They might have gone on kissing indefinitely, for now that they had started, there seemed no good reason for ever stopping, but long before the novelty was even beginning to pall, the door had been thrown open and Jesse had appeared, carrying a trayful of dirty dinner plates. (It could have been worse: it could have been Chris.) Mag-

gie and Sebastian sprang apart as if they had been caught
in some nefarious act. Jesse, plainly unprepared for such
a scene, said: "Oh!" And then, speedily recovering: "I
just came to tell you that the coast is clear. . . . We've
reached the Christmas pudding stage. Unless, of course,
you'd rather stay out here and cuddle—"

Even if they would, they couldn't have, not now.
Meekly they went back with Jesse to the dining room.
Dot gave them a bright smile. Pa said: "Ah! Here's our
young vegetarian friend. I hope he's not teetotal as
well?"

Ma, with asperity, said: "Of course he isn't. He drank
last night, didn't he? Or were you asleep? Chris, fill
Sebastian's glass." (Ma's public manners did tend to be
marginally less repulsive than Pa's. Only marginally, but
still that was something.)

Chris picked up the wine bottle and leaned across the
table. He caught Maggie's eye and winked; with Chris
that was the nearest you ever came to getting an apology
—and translated, it meant, I am prepared to forgive you
if you are prepared to forgive me—and ruffled Sebastian's hair and said: "Come on, Brains! Drink up." At
least he said it quite pleasantly.

As for the shower of salt all over the carpet, nobody
mentioned it.

Next morning Maggie and Sebastian, with Chris and
Jesse, and, of course, Bess, who was never left out of
anything if she could possibly wheedle her way in, drove
in Jesse's little old clapped-out motorcar to somewhere
called the Lickey Hills, which, according to Ma, was one
of the local beauty spots. After yesterday's contretemps
at the dinner table Chris had been making a determined

effort. He now thumped Sebastian on the back with a "Move it, move it! Pick up those legs, you vile boy!" and shot off up the hill with Bess and Sebastian in hot pursuit. That was all very well, thought Maggie, and she was glad Chris was behaving decently for once, but it meant that she was left alone with Jesse, and she wasn't quite sure, just at this moment, that she wanted to be. He was bound to ask awkward questions like—

"So how's the shorthand-typing going?"

Like, so how's the shorthand-typing going? . . . She had known that he would. Ma and Pa had preserved a stony silence on the subject, and Dot was too wrapped up with the baby, but someone, sometime, had to inquire.

"It's all right," she said, striving to inject a note of enthusiasm. She didn't really feel inclined to talk about shorthand-typing. It was, after all, but a means to an end. "Did I tell you," she said, brightly, "that Sebastian and I have a cat?"

"A cat? You and Sebastian?"

"We found her up a tree—well, I found her up a tree. It was dreadful; she was half-starved. We think someone must have thrown her out because she was pregnant. Sebastian said she'd had kittens quite recently. We looked over the marsh to see if we could find a nest or anything, but there wasn't any trace. Sebastian thinks they probably died. He says she probably didn't have enough milk for them."

"Sebastian seems to know quite a lot about animals."

"Yes, he does—wild ones, too. Not just domestic."

"And how much do you know about Sebastian?"

She stiffened, automatically on the defensive. "About Sebastian? Why?"

"No particular reason. You seemed quite close—I just wondered."

He hadn't just wondered. She didn't believe it.

"I hope you're not going to try telling me I shouldn't go around with him."

"Why should I try telling you that?"

"Chris has."

"Oh, well! Chris. Chris has a pretty low tolerance threshold. Anyone not exactly in the mold—"

"Just because Sebastian isn't in the mold, it doesn't mean there's anything wrong with him."

"Of course it doesn't. I wasn't implying that it did."

So why? What was the point?

"Sebastian's only trouble," said Maggie, "is that he *cares* about things. Sometimes he might perhaps care a bit too much, but that's surely better than not caring at all?"

"Undoubtedly," said Jesse.

"He just gets a bit oversensitive. He can't shut things out like the rest of us."

"No," said Jesse.

"Things that we might just forget about . . . they really bug him. He really gets unhappy over them. Then he goes and does something or says something, and people like Chris say he's balmy."

"You don't want to take too much notice of Chris."

"Well, I don't, as a rule, but I loathe it when he's so— so bloody *fascist.* What harm has Sebastian ever done him?"

"Ruffled his conscience perhaps?"

"Yes—like when he spoke up about that Speech Day person that was a Nazi and everybody ratted on him. *He* got the sack, and *they* all sat back and said nothing. I know he might have been a bit extreme, but—"

"That," said Jesse, "was ever the problem."

Of course. She was forgetting: Jesse had been at Trinity when Chris and Sebastian were still snot-nosed brats, hadn't he? Rather shyly she said: "What was he like at school? Sebastian?"

There was a pause while Jesse thought back; then with a slight smile he said: "Excitable."

"Yes, that's how he still is—when he's not being depressed. He gets these awful moods when he's all locked away inside himself. Chris says he's just putting it on. He says he just does it to get attention, but he doesn't. I mean, he *does* get attention, but he doesn't do it on purpose. It's something he can't help. And I *know* he can be tiresome, but at least he's never mean, or spiteful, or backbiting. He'd never do anything to hurt anyone. However maddening he is, you can't help feeling fond of him."

"No, so I observed!"

She blushed (for the second time in a week).

"Well, anyway, Dot likes him. She thinks he's nice."

"And so do you, so that makes two . . . he obviously has something that appeals to the maternal instinct— hey!" Jesse put up both hands to defend himself. "Knock it off, Amazon! I've got to be on duty tomorrow morning . . . I'd like to get back in one piece!"

12

On New Year's Eve they went to a party given by Peter and Jimmy in their apartment on the ground floor. It had been touch and go whether Sebastian would make it. He had been hovering all day on the brink of one of his depressions, lying on his bed with his hands clasped behind his neck, just staring up at the ceiling and refusing even to grunt an acknowledgment when Maggie put her head around the door and urged him to bestir himself. She had tried everything she knew, from sympathetic coaxing to brisk, no-nonsense "pull yourself together." None of it had the least effect. Sebastian in a really depressive fit was Sebastian impenetrable.

She had asked him, once, what it was that made him so desperately unhappy. "Is it something you're scared of? Something you're scared is going to happen? Or is it something that *has* happened? Something that happened years ago?"

Her attempts at amateur psychiatry fell sadly flat; either he couldn't tell her, or he wouldn't. She was inclined to think that he himself scarcely knew. It frightened her, sometimes, the grip that it had on him, it was so all-enveloping, it swamped him so utterly; yet, deep down, it was hard to escape the conviction that he *could* snap out of it if only he would. If only he were prepared to make that little bit of extra effort.

On New Year's Eve he actually did so; at the last minute, against all expectations, he suddenly cheered up and seemed prepared to enjoy himself. Maggie squeezed his hand gratefully (she had not been looking forward to going on her own).

"You see?" she said. "It's not so bad."

Alas, it didn't last. Long before "Auld Lang Syne" she was recognizing the familiar symptoms—the nervous gesture of pushing back his hair, the trapped expression that appeared in his eyes—and she knew that just like that other time, at Mick and Paula's, the noise was beginning to confuse him. Making kaleidoscopes in his brain.

She wasn't very surprised when shortly before midnight, with the same sort of urgent desperation as one might say: "I'm going to be sick" or "I need to lie down," he announced that he had to get out and get some air.

Her heart sank.

"Do you want me to come with you?" she said, but he only looked at her rather vacantly, as if he weren't quite sure who she was, and shook his head and muttered something that she couldn't catch.

She thought afterward, when he had been away for more than half an hour, that she really ought to have gone with him. It wasn't his fault that he—Her mind sought for the right word. That he was . . . what? Oversensitive? Emotionally insecure? Not mentally robust? That was it. Some people weren't physically robust, Sebastian wasn't mentally so. He might be clever, academically, but he wasn't . . . *stable.* He allowed himself to be too easily knocked off-balance. It was boring, and it was tiresome, but she was supposed to be his friend.

On the other hand, it was warm indoors and extremely cold outside. Especially if he had gone over the marsh— and that was all affectation anyway. If he needed fresh air, why not go for a quick run around the block? That would soon clear the cobwebs. All this gazing at the water and maundering about death. He really ought to take a grip on himself.

She glanced rather wistfully around the room. She saw Val, as usual, entwined with Shalid; they looked as if they had been stuck together with glue. Mick and Paula were sprawled over each other on the sofa. Jimmy was dancing cheek to cheek with one of his harem. She remembered Christmas night in the kitchen with Sebastian. The way it had felt when he had kissed her. Their lips pressed together and their arms wrapped around each other and their bodies touching. The warmth and the mystery and the excitement. Oh, why couldn't he always be like that? Why couldn't he just be *normal?*

He came back in the end, but it was too late by then. The party was over, and everyone was leaving. As luck would have it, he walked straight into Val, wearing her fur coat. He grabbed at the arm of it, feeling the texture between his fingers.

"Is this real animal fur?"

Val tossed her head.

"I should hope so! The amount it cost."

"You ought not to wear real animal fur. You're only—"

"Get lost!" Val jerked her arm away from him. "I shall wear whatever I choose to wear."

I know how you feel, thought Maggie. *I know just how you feel.* . . .

The next day was Saturday. Usually, on a Saturday, they were down in the square by eight o'clock selling newspapers. She had thought that today they might possibly have been allowed a little respite, considering it was New Year and they had been up until the small hours, but no, not a bit of it. At a quarter to eight he came hammering and crashing at her door, demanding to know if she was ready. Ready! She hadn't even opened her eyes.

She opened them now and saw at once that it was raining. Not just raining but pouring. She also saw that it was only a quarter to eight. She flumped across the room in her pajamas, opened the door a crack, and said: "Do we have to?"

"Of course we have to! What's the matter with you?"

"A, I'm still asleep and B, it's coming down in buckets."

"So it's coming down in buckets . . . so that doesn't stop people from slaughtering animals, does it? If you're fighting for a cause, you're fighting for a cause. You don't let a little thing like the weather put you off. Think of all those seal pups clubbed to death. Think of—"

"Oh, go *away*," said Maggie. "Come back in ten minutes. I'll let you know."

By eight o'clock, huddled into two layers of sweater and her duffle coat, with her feet pushed into boots and her hands enclosed in woolly mittens and her old school scarf wound thrice about her neck, she was stumping down the road in the teeth of a howling gale. Sebastian strode purposefully at her side, his bundle of newspapers buttoned into his jacket. His hands were bare, and she knew for a fact that his boots leaked.

"This is ridiculous!" she said as blasts of icy wind cut across them from the marsh. "We ought at least to get a bus."

"Would," said Sebastian, "if I had the bread."

"I've got bread. I've got next term's allowance."

"So you get one. Go and have a coffee. I'll see you there."

"I can't, if you won't. . . . Oh, come on! I'll pay the fare."

"No, you won't."

"Yes, I will."

"No, you *won't*. I can't keep sponging off you. I already owe you a fiver."

"Doesn't matter."

"It does matter. How do I know if I'm ever going to be able to pay it back?"

"Well, of course you'll be able to pay it back. Just as soon as you get a job." If ever he did get a job. "You could have had one last week if only you weren't so fussy."

Sebastian frowned.

"I told you . . . I'm not working for an organization that exists solely to make profit."

Oh, no! Of course not. They all knew profit was a dirty word. We couldn't go against our principles, could we? We couldn't soil our conscience helping someone to make *money*. Not that we had any objection to borrowing a fiver out of Pa's ill-gotten gains. Maggie looked up at him in sudden irritation.

"So what *are* you going to do?"

"Stand firm. What are you?"

"Me?" She was indignant; the discussion wasn't about her. "You know what I'm going to do."

"Go into an office."

"So what's wrong with that?"

"Swelling the coffers of capitalism."

"So?"

"So it's immoral."

"Immoral!" She poured as much scorn into the word as she could; it wasn't very much since the wind whipped most of it away. "What's immoral," she shouted, "about making a living?"

"Everything, when it's at other people's expense . . . oil companies, tobacco companies, multinationals—*super*-markets. Where do you think their profits come from? Thin air? You can't make profit out of nothing. There's only one way you can make it, and that's by taking it away from someone else."

"Oh, shut up!" said Maggie. She didn't feel like entering an argument with Sebastian just at this moment, and anyway, suppose she went into an office that was a charity? Oxfam, or Amnesty International, or something? They didn't all have to be industry and commerce.

"Society shouldn't be run on the basis of profit. It should be run on the basis of need. From each according to his ability, to each according to—"

"Oh, shut *up!*" said Maggie.

They reached the bottom of the hill and turned right, along Drovers' Road, toward the High Street. It was at this point, as a rule, that Maggie took Sebastian very firmly by the arm and crossed him over to the other side, for in Drovers' Road there was a butcher's shop, and butcher's shops and Sebastian were better, in her experience, kept as far apart as possible. Today, what with the

wind and the rain and him still yelling Marxist dogma
down her ear, she quite forgot about the perils ahead.
Even so, all might not yet have been completely lost, for
Sebastian once started on one of his diatribes tended to
become oblivious even to butcher's shops. So long as he
was ranting, she could safely steer him past a dozen or
more. Unfortunately what she could not steer him past
was a refrigerated van full of carcasses. She saw it just a
fraction of a second too late. Before she could swing Sebastian in the other direction, a white-coated man with a
shrouded but unmistakable shape slung across his shoulder had stepped right out in front of them. Useless expecting Sebastian to turn a blind eye; he was constitu-
tionally incapable of it. She snatched at his arm, trying to
hustle him past—"Come on! Don't stand gaping, we'll
lose our spot"—but he might have been stone-deaf for
all the effect that it had. He was obviously in one of his
manic crusading moods. What if the Salvation Army or
the Socialist Workers did steal a march? There was more
pressing business to be attended to here.

Sebastian disappeared into the butcher's shop in the
wake of the carcass. Already she could hear his voice
raised in exhortation. A blue-rinsed lady with a small
dog tucked under her arm had frozen, mouth agape, one
hand still stretched out to receive her change. Even as
Maggie watched, Sebastian tore the dog away from her.
He held it aloft, thrusting it into her face.

"How would you like to see *him* put through a mincing
machine? How would you like to see *him* hanging up
there with his throat slit? Why eat one sort of animal if
you won't eat another? They've got just as much right to
live as he has, haven't they?"

Maggie cringed. She could feel her cheeks pulsating.

She knew she ought to go in and haul him out, but it was no good, she just couldn't. She felt a strong temptation to turn and run.

Her feet wouldn't move. Not in one direction or the other. She stood where she was, glowing like a light bulb. Why did he do these things? God, why did he *do* them?

Suddenly, in a rush, Sebastian was on the pavement beside her—propelled there by the butcher.

"Out! Get out! Go on—the pair of you! Move!"

Even then he wouldn't. Even then he had to try to argue, had to take out one of his stickers and try to plaster it onto the shopfront. A couple of middle-aged women with shopping baskets audibly muttered as they passed. She caught the words "young hooligans" and "ought to be locked up." From the grocer's over the road came a hoarse shout of "Fetch the law, mate! I would!" Maggie wanted to die. She wanted to lie down right where she was and die.

"Right! That does it!" The butcher caught Sebastian by the shoulders. He spun him around and hurled him across the pavement at Maggie. "Either you clear off and don't come back, or it's names and addresses, and heaven help the pair of you!"

Maggie felt a surge of resentment. "What am I suppose to have done?"

"You're with him, aren't you? Well, then, get him out of here—go on! Shove off!"

They did so. The butcher's voice echoed up the street behind them: "And you can count yourselves lucky!"

Maggie waited only until they were safely around the corner, then turned on Sebastian in savage fury.

"I'm sick of it! I'm *sick* of it! Why do you have to keep

doing it? *Every*where, all the *time*—why can't you learn to control yourself? Why can't you *think* before you act? You haven't any discipline; that's your whole trouble! It's the very reason why you antagonize everybody, why sooner or later you get everyone's back up, why they get *bored* by you, why—"

On she went, and on. Screeching like a virago. And Sebastian just standing there, taking it.

"Where do you think you're going in life? What do you think's going to happen to you? You get chucked out of school, you get chucked out of university—"

He winced slightly at that, but still he didn't say anything. Later—weeks later—she was to wonder why he hadn't. Now she only went on screaming.

"Always making a spectacle of yourself, always making yourself a laughingstock. Making *both* of us a laughingstock. Well, I've had it, do you hear me? I have *had* it. H-A-D, *had* it. Just because *you* don't care if everyone thinks you're balmy, it doesn't mean to say you have to make them think *I* am. From now on you can go sell your stupid newspapers by yourself. I don't see why *I* should be labeled a freak."

At the stop over the road a bus was pulling in. She turned and plunged toward it through the traffic. Her heart was hammering, power drills thudding through her head. *Bloody* Sebastian. Sebastian was *bloody*. Her legs, as she climbed onto the platform, were all wobbly. They were still wobbly when she got off again at the top of Station Road. The hood of her duffle had blown off, and her hair was soaking. Everything was soaking. She would like to have *murdered* him.

Sunday was waiting on the gatepost, loudly demanding to be let in. Maggie scooped her up and carried her through into the hall. The post had been delivered. There was a library card for Sandy Grace, two airmail letters for Jimmy, something that looked nasty, in a brown envelope, for Mick, and a letter postmarked Leeds, addressed baldly to M. Easter, in writing which she recognized as belonging to Chris. She wondered rather sourly what had prompted him to communicate. It wasn't her birthday, was it?

Upstairs in her room she lit the gas fire for Sunday, who promptly set about grooming herself, draped her wet clothes over the plastic clothesline donated by Dot ("It's not the sort of thing one ever thinks of, but you'll find it comes in very handy, believe me"), and made herself a cup of coffee. Then she sat down and opened Chris's letter.

Chris had never written her a letter in his life before. He still hadn't—just two short sentences carelessly scribbled on the back of an old Students' Union card: "Sorry I was rotten about old Brains. He's not so bad."

Huh! Maggie crumpled the card into a ball and hurled it vehemently across the room at the wastepaper basket. Trust Chris. He would have to go send her a note like that at a time like this, wouldn't he? Just when she was trying so hard to convince herself that Sebastian was absolutely hellish—well, he *was* absolutely hellish. *Absolutely* hellish.

Downstairs someone rang at her doorbell. If that was the idiot now, without his key—

It wasn't. It was Val—very chic and elegant in knee-length boots and belted raincoat, with a flowered umbrella in the shape of a pagoda. And in spite of the wind, not a beautiful red-gold hair out of place. Maggie said: "Oh. It's you."

"I looked for you in the square, but you weren't there. Sebastian said he thought you'd probably have come home."

"Yes. . . . Is he there?"

"Well, obviously," said Val, "or I couldn't have spoken to him, could I? Have you had a row or something?"

There was too much eagerness in her tone. Maggie said: "No. Sebastian doesn't have rows. Are you going to come in?"

"Only for a second. I'm meeting Shalid. I came to ask you something."

Guardedly, as she led the way upstairs, Maggie said: "What?"

"I want you to make up a foursome—in fact, you've *got* to make up a foursome because if you don't, Abdul won't come, and it won't be nearly as much fun as if we all went together. That stupid woman Jane Hirst was *supposed* to be coming. Now she's gone and backed out at the last moment. Rang me up just before breakfast, if you please. Honestly, people are so unreliable. How does she think she's going to be able to hold down a secretarial post if she carries on like this? Anyway—"

Anyway, she had thought immediately of Maggie. Good old Maggie. *She* would fill the gap.

"You will, won't you? You will say yes? Abdul's always asking about you. He can't understand what went wrong that first evening."

"Nothing went wrong. He just didn't seem terribly struck on me."

"You didn't give him much of a chance, chasing around after Sebastian. And if he wasn't struck, he wouldn't keep asking."

"Huh!"

"Oh, please, Maggie, do say yes!"

"You haven't yet told me when it is."

"Tonight."

"To*night?*"

"Well, what else have you got on? What do you usually do on a Saturday?"

Usually on a Saturday she did things with Sebastian. Sometimes, when they had the money, they might go to the cinema. Other times, when people were giving parties, they might go to a party. When there weren't any parties and they didn't have any money, they would just go for a walk, or play the poetry game, or maybe make up a quiz. Tonight, because Sebastian was out of work and wouldn't borrow any more of Pa's filthy lucre and it was raining cats and dogs, they would probably just have sat indoors in front of Maggie's gas fire.

"You can't be doing anything important," urged Val.

No, it certainly couldn't be described as important. She didn't even know, after this morning, whether Sebastian would still expect it. And going dancing at the Pavilion was on any count more exciting than sitting indoors playing the poetry game. She wavered.

"Well—I suppose—"

"What were you *actually* doing?"

"Only seeing Sebastian."

"Well, you can put *him* off," said Val. "He's bats anyway. Probably doesn't even know which day of the week it is."

Val could be very tactless at times. Very stupid. (Vain and shallow and petty-minded . . .) Did she not realize that she had almost had victory within her grasp?

"If he didn't know what day of the week it was,"

snapped Maggie, "he wouldn't be in the square selling papers, would he?"

"Oh, you know what I mean!"

Yes. What she meant was that if Jane Hirst stood someone up at the last minute, it was unreliable, but if Maggie stood Sebastian up at the last minute, it didn't matter because it was only Sebastian.

"Let's face it," said Val, "he is stark raving bonkers."

"That doesn't stop him from being a human being, does it?"

"If human it can be called. . . . He's certainly not *normal.*"

Maggie wrestled a moment with her temper. Between her teeth she said: "He does have feelings, you know."

"Oh, I'm sure."

"Well, he does!"

"Yes, I'm sure. I said."

"As a matter of fact, for your information, Sebastian has a great deal more in the way of feelings than some people I could name. . . . *He* wouldn't go around saying a person was stark raving bonkers behind their back."

Val smiled sweetly. "Would you rather I said it to his face?"

"It might perhaps be better if you didn't say it at all."

"Oh, for heaven's sake!" Noise of impatience and contempt. "What's happened to you? You used to be fun. Now all you ever do is preach, and prate, and lecture people."

"Maybe because I've started thinking about things."

"Well, heaven preserve *me* from it, if that's what it does to you."

"I don't think there's much danger," said Maggie, "of your ever thinking about things."

Val colored. Very deliberately she walked over to the hearth and picked up her flowered umbrella.

"I might as well go," she said. "I'm obviously wasting my time."

"Look, if you'd given me a bit more notice—"

"Oh, don't worry! I won't have any difficulty finding anyone. I just thought I ought to give you first chance—seeing as we used to be friends. And seeing as I felt sorry for you." She opened the door. "Stuck with Sebastian."

When Val had gone, Maggie thought about Sebastian. She thought about him while she made the bed and did yesterday's washing up and brushed the tangles out of her hair with the brush that he had commandeered for the cat. The awful thing was that she knew—she just knew—that if she were to go down to the square now and behave as if nothing had ever happened, Sebastian would do the same. Even though she'd bawled at him and been as vile as she knew how. He wouldn't bear any grudge. He wouldn't retaliate. Sebastian never did. No matter how impassioned he became, he never lost his temper. He never said things on purpose to hurt or belittle; he was as gentle with people as he was with animals. She remembered one time before Christmas when she'd had the curse, really crippling, so bad she had wanted to scream and roll about the floor in hoops. Chris always told her it was "all in the mind" and "if you didn't *expect* it to happen, then it wouldn't." Chris was never sympathetic about anything which he hadn't experienced for himself. Neither was Val. What Val said was, if it didn't get her like that, why should it get Maggie? Sebastian had been really kind, really understanding. He had admittedly suggested that a brisk run across the marsh might do her a world of good, but when she had grizzled, in her feeble way, that all she wanted to do was huddle in front of the gas fire and moan, he hadn't insisted or told her not to be so wet; he had simply huddled in front of the gas fire with her, telling her terrible jokes to try to cheer her up.

"Hear the one about the cannibal who passed his mate in the jungle?"

"Did what?"

"Passed his mate in the—"

"Oh, *no! Se*bastian!"

Sebastian's jokes were always terrible. She sometimes thought he got them out of cracker boxes. But at least he had tried, and never once had he accused her of ruining the evening, even though they had been supposed to be going to a party. Chris would have dragged her there whether she liked it or not.

She looked out the window. The rain had turned to sleet, slashing bullets of ice—and Sebastian in the square with his leaking boots and no gloves.

With a sigh, Maggie pulled on her sodden duffle coat. She turned off the gas, made a nest for Sunday in the bedclothes.

"You stay there," she said.

Sunday didn't need to be told. She had been out once; she wasn't going out a second time. Maggie had also been out once; she supposed it was her own fault if now she had to go out again. She knew, after all, what Sebastian was like. She knew he couldn't help it. It was no use going on at him.

She took the bus back down the hill, into the center of town. Sebastian was standing where he always stood, between the *Morning Star* and the Rotary Club, except that this morning, the weather being what it was, the

Rotary Club had chickened out. The *Morning Star* was still there. Just the *Morning Star* and Sebastian. He had the collar of his jacket turned up, and his hands dug deep into his pockets, with the newspapers tucked under his arm, and was moving from foot to foot in an effort to keep warm. When he saw Maggie, he looked at her uncertainly. "Did Val find you? I told her I th—"

"Yes. She found me." Maggie stationed herself at his side. "Come on, then." She nudged him. "Give us some papers. . . . Sooner we get rid of them, sooner we can get back."

13

"The trouble with James Bond," said Maggie, "is that it's sexist."

"*And* racist."

"And elitist?"

"Absolutely."

"It's funny, one never really noticed it when one was younger."

"That's because one just accepted whatever was pumped into one."

"I'm not quite sure I'm really grabbed by it any-more—"

"I should hope you're not. I should hope I've taught you better than *that.*"

"So why did we go?"

Sebastian shrugged. "Nothing else on."

No, she supposed that there wasn't—and they had had to go somewhere. They had had to go somewhere, to celebrate Sebastian's first pay packet. He had started work a week ago in the parks and gardens department of the local authority. It didn't pay very much, but at least it was out of doors, and no one could accuse it of operating on a profit basis.

They walked back up the hill, hand in hand, in the February drizzle. It had been one of those weekends when Sebastian had been so blissfully normal that it was hard to believe he could ever be anything other. He hadn't harangued anyone; he hadn't become depressive; he hadn't even stuck any stickers onto other people's property. On Friday he had given Maggie back her five pounds, and they had promptly spent it on going to the Pavilion with Mick and Paula and eating a Chinese meal afterward. On Saturday there had been a party just across the road, where some drama students lived. It hadn't been a terribly swinging sort of party, but at least Sebastian had stayed the course. It had been one occasion when Maggie hadn't had to gaze wistfully at other people enjoying themselves and wonder how on earth she had ever come to get mixed up with Sebastian. Tonight he had taken her to see a James Bond, and even if the film itself hadn't quite lived up to childhood memories—because what, after all, could you be expected to know when you were only thirteen or fourteen?—they had nevertheless sat in the dark and held hands, the sort of nice, ordinary, everyday thing that you couldn't very often do with Sebastian because usually he was too busy being overexcited or manically depressed.

They reached the top of the hill and called for Sunday, who usually sat on the gatepost, waiting. This evening she wasn't there.

"Where is she?" said Sebastian.

"Probably gone indoors. You know what she's like—first hint of rain, and that's it."

They opened the front door and called, but Sunday didn't appear. Sebastian went upstairs, and Maggie went down to the basement, but not a sign of her.

"Let's try outside again."

They tried outside again. Sebastian whistled his special Sunday whistle, to which, as a rule, she would re-
spond instantly, no matter where she was. She had even
been known to abandon a mouse chase when Sebastian
whistled. Tonight there was only silence. No rustling of
bushes, no self-important chirrup.

"We can't just leave her," said Sebastian.

They walked up and down the road, whistling and
calling, looking into people's gardens, peering into trees:
no Sunday.

"I hope to God she hasn't got run over."

"Of course she hasn't," said Maggie stoutly. She
wasn't having Sebastian go to pieces on her. "You know
she never crosses the road."

"Then where's she got to?"

"She could be anywhere. Probably stalking something
or spending the night on the tiles."

"But she wouldn't—she doesn't! She always comes."

"Cats never do anything *always.*"

"They come for their food always."

"Not if they've just gorged themselves on a diet of
fresh mice. . . . Look, if she doesn't want to come, then
nothing's going to make her. We're just wasting our time.
Let her stay out; it won't hurt her for once. It's not as if
it's freezing, and anyway, there's plenty of cover. Oh,
come on, Sebastian! Cats do stay out all night."

He pushed a lock of hair out of his eyes. "I'll just have
one more look. You go on in."

She hesitated. "You won't be long?"

"No, I—I'll just—just take a wander."

With some misgivings Maggie walked back up the
front steps. She didn't like leaving him to go off on his

own, but it was already half past eleven, and first period tomorrow old Everton had threatened them with a shorthand speed test. Normally Maggie wouldn't have given two straws for a shorthand speed test, but it was a strange thing, ever since she and Val had become—not hostile, exactly, but certainly disenchanted—an element of rivalry had grown up which had never been there before. Before, Maggie had been quite happy that Val should walk off with all the shorthand-typing honors while she herself was classified as "stupid." Now, suddenly, it had become important that she should demonstrate to everyone that all this shorthand-typing stuff was just child's play, anyone could do it if she set her mind to it.

Rather surprisingly she was discovering that anyone could. All she had needed was the spur (albeit a rather ignoble one? Sebastian said that cooperation, not competition, should be the guiding light of the new society). Be that as it may, she had astonished everybody, including herself, by coming out on top in last week's test: 110 words per minute, and she had read every single one of them back. It seemed a rather paltry sort of achievement compared with others she could think of, but at least she had done it. At least she had proved that she could if she wanted.

In any case everyone *knew* that cats liked the occasional night out. There wasn't any need for all this tramping the streets. Sunday would come in when she felt like coming—probably at two o'clock in the morning, and that would be her hard luck. Maybe it would teach her a lesson. She either came when she was called or got shut out.

Maggie lit the gas fire, climbed into her pajamas,

cleaned her teeth, and put the kettle on. She made a cup of coffee. It was almost midnight. Surely he couldn't *still* be out there? She flung open the window and leaned over the sill, getting wet. It was too dark to see very much. Perhaps he had found the cat and come back in, except that surely he would have stopped off to tell her. She closed the window with a bang. Sebastian really was such a *nuisance.*

Downstairs she stood at the front door in her dressing gown for almost five minutes. The street outside was empty. She went back up and knocked at Sebastian's door, just in case, but as she had expected, there was no reply. He obviously was still out there. Well, there was nothing she could do. If he wanted to spend half the night roaming the streets, that was his problem.

Maybe it was, but she still couldn't sleep. For twenty minutes she tossed and turned, then finally switched on the light and tried reading. That wasn't much good either. Sebastian had given her some turgid rubbish all about the workings of capitalism, and it was boring her silly. What she needed was a good meaty novel. A good *yarn,* as her English mistress at Tennyson had used to say. "If you want a good yarn, try *Moby Dick.'*

She had, and that had bored her, too. But even *Moby Dick* would be better than the workings of capitalism.

Fitfully she dozed. A sudden noise awoke her—the creaking of floorboards outside. She looked at her traveling clock, and it said twenty-five past one. *Sebastian?*

She padded across the room and opened the door about half an inch. He was on his way up the stairs. She whispered to him: "Did you find her?"

He turned. His hair was plastered to his forehead, his jeans clinging damply to his legs. He shook his head.

"No."

"You haven't been out there all this time?"

"I went over the marsh. I thought—perhaps—" He pushed his hair away. "Perhaps she—might have—gone there—"

"Oh, *Sebastian!*"

"I c-couldn't help it. I c-couldn't just l-leave her. I had to t-try."

"But you're soaking! You're—oh, come here!" She seized him by the hand, dragging him back down the stairs. He came obediently. She led him across the room, sat him down by the hearth. "Put the fire on—no, it's all right, don't bother, I'll do it." Sebastian obviously wasn't in a fit state to do anything. He seemed disoriented, as one in a daze. He oughtn't to have animals, she thought. If anything had happened to that cat—

A shiver ran through her. Sebastian was also shivering. He knelt before the fire, with the rain running in rivulets down his face, trickling off the end of his nose, his jeans making wet patches on the hearth rug. Maggie threw a towel at him.

"Dry your hair. I'll make some coffee."

She made the coffee, but Sebastian didn't dry his hair. He just went on kneeling in front of the fire, clutching at the towel and doing nothing with it.

"Sebastian—"

He looked up at her.

"She'll come back. She'll be all right. You'll see."

She took the towel from him and dried his hair. Then she pulled a blanket off the bed and said: "Get out of those wet clothes; you'll catch pneumonia." Pa had told her often enough that one didn't "catch" pneumonia from sitting about in wet clothes, but still, she thought, it couldn't be good for you. If nothing else, it made you feel clammy and uncomfortable.

"Come on!" She took hold of his sweater and tugged. "Do something!" Zombielike, he stretched up his arms. She heaved the sweater over his head, wrung it out in the basin and hung it over Dot's plastic clothesline. *"And* jeans—*and* boots—*and* socks."

She hung the jeans and the socks next to the sweater, stood the boots on a sheet of newspaper beneath the table. Sebastian sat huddled in his blanket. She hadn't realized until now just how terribly thin he was. He reminded her of photographs she had seen of prisoners of war.

"Drink your coffee," she said.

He picked up the mug, but he didn't drink. She didn't have to ask him what he was thinking about. He was thinking about Sunday—Sunday being run over, lying injured, being frightened, being in pain. He was doing one of his torturing acts.

"Sebastian, stop it!" she said. She took the coffee away from him, set it back in the hearth. "Just don't do it—don't *let* yourself."

"I c-can't help it."

"You can help it! Concentrate! Think of something else. Think of—"

"I c-can't!" With a convulsive movement he threw himself onto Maggie's bed, burying his face in her pillow. "I j-just know that s-something t-terrible has h-happened to her. I keep s-seeing her—"

"Well, don't! Sebastian, *don't!"* She spoke as commandingly as she knew how. It had worked wonders with the juniors at school; it didn't seem to have any effect on Sebastian.

She sat back on her heels, frowning, frustrated. All very well possessing common sense, but she had the feeling one needed rather more than common sense when dealing with a person like Sebastian. One needed . . . knowledge. Knowledge of how best to treat him. Whether to be Dot-like and show sympathy, or whether to be stern and unyielding and tell him to snap out of it. She would willingly do either—if only she *knew*. To give way to Dot-like impulses and put her arms about him might only be encouraging him to further self-indulgence, yet, on the other hand, a short, sharp lecture delivered to someone who quite genuinely couldn't help himself—that surely could be of no use.

"Sebastian—" She crawled over him onto the other side of the bed and squeezed herself into the narrow space that was left between him and the wall. "Do be rational! You know far more about cats than I do, and even *I* know they can go off for days at a time. It doesn't mean anything's happened to her. She's probably just gone hunting. But she's old enough to know where she lives. It's not as if she were a kitten—and she wouldn't let anyone pick her up, so you don't have to worry about *that*. No one's going to have stolen her. . . . I bet when you go out in the morning, the first thing you'll see is her sitting there on the gatepost, preening herself. Please, Sebastian." She rubbed her cheek against his shoulder. "Do try. Try really *hard*. Try playing the poetry game . . . like if I said, *'Shall I compare thee to a summer's day?'* "

No response.

" 'SHALL I COMPARE THEE TO A SUMMER'S DAY?' " Maggie shook him. "Come on!"

" *'Sumer is icumen in, Lhude sing cuccu—'* " It came reluctantly, but it came. " *'Groweth sed, and bloweth med, And springth the wude nu. . . .'* "

"All right, you don't have to show off. . . . I shall say, *'Now is the winter of our discontent . . .'* "

" *'Winter is icumen in, Lhude sing Goddamm.'* "

She blinked. "You what? Don't mumble!"

Sebastian rolled over onto his back.

" *'Winter is icumen in, Lhude sing Goddamm, Raineth drop and staineth slop, And how the wind doth ramm! Sing: Goddamm.'* "

She looked at him. He grinned. "Ezra Pound. Go on—your turn."

How long they played the poetry game she had no idea, but at some stage she must evidently have fallen asleep, for the next thing she knew she was sitting up in bed with a start. "What—"

"I heard her. Downstairs."

The door clicked as Sebastian opened it. Thank goodness for that, thought Maggie. Now perhaps they would all be able to get some rest. She put up a hand and switched off the bedside light—the fire had long since gone—struggled out of her dressing gown, pulled the covers over her head, and collapsed in a heap.

Seconds later—Or was it minutes? Was it an hour?—she swam back to the surface to find that Sebastian had returned. He was standing there in his underpants looking like a skeleton. What did he want now?

"It wasn't her—" His voice broke. "I thought that it was . . . but it wasn't."

"Oh, *no!*" Maggie groaned. Was there never to be any peace? She screwed up her eyes. "What are you doing?"

"Getting dressed."

"What for?"

"I thought I'd—just—go over the road—"

She sprang bolt upright. "You are not going over the road! Don't be so stupid! You've already got wet through once. What's the matter with you? For crying out loud, it's only a *cat*. Cats can look after *themselves*. Just get into bed and go to sleep!"

She flung herself back down again. There was a pause while Sebastian stood, undecided, with one leg in and one leg out of his damp jeans. Determinedly Maggie humped herself over onto her side and closed her eyes. Let him get on with it. If he wanted to go roaming the marsh in search of a cat that was almost certainly tucked up somewhere, snoring its head off in a bed of leaves—

"Maggie?"

"Mm?"

"Do you really think she's all right?"

Well, at least he had decided against going over the marsh. She crammed herself against the wall to make room. "Course I do."

"Really?"

"Really."

"You're not just saying it? Just to—"

"Oh, Sebastian!" She turned back toward him. His feet were cold from having been all the way downstairs without any shoes. She curled up her toes. "You're freezing— you are an idiot! Did you go right outside?"

"I had to—I had to make sure—"

"Just stop worrying. She'll be back. Try to go to sleep."

For a few minutes there was silence. Maggie closed her eyes again. She had never been in bed with a man before, but being with Sebastian didn't feel like being in bed with a man. Sebastian was just Sebastian. They didn't have that sort of relationship.

She had *thought* they didn't have that sort of relationship. She supposed, looking back, she ought to have known better.

"Sebastian, knock it off," she said.

She didn't feel like that sort of thing at this hour of the morning. Three o'clock or whatever it was. In any case, bed wasn't the place for it—not unless you intended it to lead somewhere, and she didn't. It wasn't the moment for new experiences.

"Look, just pack it in," she said.

That was the trouble with men. Val had discovered it long since: "Only ever think of one thing. It gets so *tedious.*" Of course, that had been when Val was younger. She probably felt different now. Val had grown up in all sorts of ways.

"Sebastian, I said pack it *in,*" said Maggie. She wriggled away from him, but there wasn't much room for maneuver in one small sofa bed. She kicked at him crossly. "Go to sleep."

One didn't expect Sebastian to behave like an oaf. Other people might, but not Sebastian. Sebastian was gentle and sensitive and liked poetry. He ought to have a soul that rose above the mere physical.

He ought to have had, but obviously he hadn't.

"Maggie, can't we?" he said.

"No!" She was outraged. How dare he? How dare he even suggest it? Why couldn't he just shut up and go to sleep? "Will you please stop it," she said, "and don't be such a *bore?* For crying out *loud.*" She flounced over onto her side, taking all the bedclothes with her. "What's the *matter* with you?"

Val might have said that even an idiot might have divined what the matter was, but Val wasn't there. She was almost beginning to wish that Sebastian wasn't either.

There was a silence; then in a subdued voice he muttered: "Sorry."

So he ought to be. Behaving like some kind of sex
maniac. Three o'clock in the morning and old Everton's
speed test looming up, and he wanted to start messing
around?

"I didn't mean to upset you."

She grunted.

"I wouldn't do anything to hurt you. Honestly."

Again she grunted.

A bit more silence; then: "Maggie?"

For crying out *loud*.

"What?"

Sebastian raised himself on an elbow. She could feel
the cold draft roaring down the bed.

"You're not asleep, are you?"

Asleep? Fat chance! Sebastian bent over her, pressing
his cheek against hers. *(And* he hadn't used those razor
blades she'd given him.)

"Maggie, I'm sorry—don't go to sleep on me! Please,
Maggie! Please don't. I won't make a nuisance of myself
. . . I promise."

She clenched her fists beneath the pillow.

"You *are* making a nuisance of yourself—just *talking.* "

"Well, then, I—I won't talk. I won't say anything. I
swear it!"

She turned her head to look at him.

"So what do you want me to stay awake for?"

Sebastian bit his lip.

"I d-don't know. I just—felt lonely."

Oh, ha-ha. Very corny. If he thought she was falling
for *that* . . .

"Look," she said, "I'm telling you, if you don't intend

to shut up and lie down, you can go away and be lonely in your own bed. I've got a speed test tomorrow; I'm not sitting up half the night playing wet nurse to you. Just because the cat chooses to go out on a spree—*honestly.*" She hauled at the bedclothes. "If you want to be neurotic, go and be neurotic somewhere else. I need my sleep."

She felt mean afterward, when he had gone. Not so much about "rejecting his advances," as Val would have put it—though a little bit mean about that, too, because she *was* supposed to be a reasonably mature adult, old enough to vote and all the rest, and let's face it, she'd been acquainted with the facts of life practically ever since she could remember. It wasn't as if she could plead ignorance. She ought to have known she was asking for trouble. Men couldn't help these things (at least she supposed they couldn't). They were just made that way, and what was so wonderful about still being a virgin anyhow? Who really cared? And even if anyone did, what did it actually matter, when you came down to it? In the overall scale of things? It didn't matter tuppence. Not when set beside the bomb and starvation and all the other ills which beset the world. But then again, that wasn't any excuse for using emotional blackmail, and she didn't feel *very* mean about saying no; it was just that she didn't feel self-righteous either. What she mainly felt mean about was kicking up all that fuss over a bit of sleep. Sleep was hardly a major issue, and if virginity didn't rate high in the overall scale, then a lousy speed test couldn't be said to rate at all.

Angrily she banged the pillow back into shape. That cat had a lot to answer for. A heck of a lot. When it deigned to turn up again, beaming all over its fat face, as

no doubt it would, she was going to give it just about the
biggest talking-to it had had in its life. There was something it needed to be told: If it were going to continue to
live with Sebastian, then it would have to learn to accept
a bit more responsibility. You couldn't subject Sebastian
to the same rough-and-ready treatment you dished out
to the rest of the world. He existed on a more precarious
equilibrium; the least little thing, and he could go plung-
ing over the edge.

For the umpteenth time that night Maggie settled her
head on the pillow. She tugged the bedclothes up to her
chin, curled her knees into her chest. *Tomorrow evening,* she
thought, *I will make it up to him.*

14

It was late when Maggie woke up next morning. In all the turmoil of the previous night she had forgotten to set the alarm, with the result that it was eight-thirty before she even opened her eyes. Her first thought was for Sebastian, her second for Sunday. Only then did she remember the Everton's speed test; it was due to start in less than fifty minutes.

Blast! That meant missing breakfast. She tore herself out of bed, pulled on last night's clothes, all crumpled and creased as they were, splashed cold water over her face, grabbed bag and coat, and ran.

There was still no sign of Sunday. It was always possible that Sebastian had found her waiting for him on the gatepost and had taken her back upstairs, but in that case he would surely have left her a note or banged on her door. Sebastian didn't bear grudges, and he must know that she would be worried. Sunday was her cat as well as his, and even if a cat *was* only a cat, you could still get attached to it, with its stupid furry face and its little, no-neck body and the great, round, owly eyes that went huge as soup plates whenever it yawned. In spite of her assurances, she couldn't help feeling a few pinpricks of anxiety. Instinctively, as she pelted down the road to the bus stop, she found her gaze raking the gutter in search of that pathetic bundle of fur that would tell its own tale. She wondered what she would do if she came upon it. She would pick it up and give it a decent burial, of course, and the speed test could go hang, but would she ever have the courage to break the news to Sebastian?

She reached the bus stop and took a grip on herself. Never mind breaking any news to Sebastian; she was *behaving* like Sebastian. Torturing herself, imagining the worst. It only went to show how fatally easy it was.

"The thing to do is think of other things." That was what she had said to Sebastian, wasn't it? Very well then.

"Winter is icumen in, Lhude sing Goddamm—"

Cats had been known to go off for weeks at a time. If it weren't for Sebastian, all these morbid notions would never have come into her head in the first place.

She reached college with seconds to spare. Val, cool and poised, with fountain pen at the ready and shorthand notebook all prepared, with the bottom right-hand corners of the page neatly folded back to facilitate quick turnover, took one look at her and said: "My, my! Someone's had a wild night. Fun and games?"

"You could put it that way," said Maggie.

"Not with Sebastian?" Val smirked. "I didn't think he was capable. . . ."

Miss Everton came in and began on her speed test without even the elementary courtesy of a warning.

"A hundred and ten words per minute. Are you ready? Right." Get set, *go.* "Heading: Industrial Report. Date: Twenty-sixth February—"

Maggie groped feverishly for her notebook, flipping it

open at random. The Everton gabbled on, like one de-
mented.

*"Increasing-profit-is-to-be-made-by-astute-middlemen-in-the-microchip-
industry—"*

Blast! That was the point of her pencil gone.

"—as Distributech, the-London-based-electronics-group—"

She snatched up another. Blunter than the bluntest of
blunt instruments.

"—proved-yesterday. It-is-in-simple-terms—"

This was ridiculous.

"—a-microchip-supermart-which-buys-silicon-chip-components—"

For crying out loud! Maggie flung down her second
pencil and clawed up her ball-point. Ball-points were
strictly forbidden, but so what?

*"—and-sells-them-at-a-profit. The-growing-list-of-industries-us-
ing-microprocessors—"*

Profit was a dirty word anyway. Sebastian said so. After all, where did profit come from? It didn't come out of
thin air. There was only one way you could make
profit. . . .

"—up-to-thirty-eight-percent-for-the-half-year-to-December-the-first—"

Needless to say, her ball-point ran out. It was that sort
of morning. She had to finish off in blunt pencil, which
made dots the size of footballs and thin strokes indistin-
guishable from thick. Val, as usual, handed in three pages
of immaculate, spider's web tracery, every outline a min-
iature work of art in its own right; Maggie handed in a
hideous scrawl of blue ball-point and blunt pencil, full of
her own personal abbreviations, which owed little or
nothing to the Pitman system of shorthand. The Everton
didn't like her writing ∴ for "therefore" and ∵ for "because." Even less did she like her writing bits of Latin
and French. She was under the impression, she said, that

Maggie had been sent here to learn Pitman's, not to perfect Easter's. Always so *sarcastic.*

After lunch they were expected to transcribe and type out what they had taken down in the morning. Even apart from the fact that Maggie couldn't decipher her own scribble ("increasing profit is made by *Aztec Metalmen*"?), she was quite unable to concentrate. There was something at the back of her mind that kept nagging at her—something that was wrong. She kept thinking it was Sunday's not coming back, but it wasn't. It was bound up with that, but it wasn't that in itself. There was something other than that, which she couldn't pin down. Whatever it was, it certainly obtruded between her and the silicon chip. Indeed, it made the silicon chip, not to mention the Pitman dot, quite fade into insignificance. Val could have all the honors this week, and welcome.

The last class of the day was office practice, when they were supposed to be learning about filing, and whether to put Marsh-Jones under *M* or *J,* which seemed to Maggie quite immaterial so long as you stuck to one or the other. She said as much to Miss Everton, who was rather cold about it and scathingly informed her that wayward individuality might be all very well for pop stars "and the like" but was quite out of place in an office.

"If we all stick to the prevailing system, we promote efficiency; if we each take our own path, it leads to muddle and chaos and finally anarchy."

So what was wrong with that? Sebastian said that anarchy was a good thing. He said it was what society should ultimately be aiming at.

"An-archy: without government. So who wants to be governed? Do *you* want to be governed? *I* don't want to be governed. Do *you* want people telling you what to do? *I* don't want people—"

"Miss Easter, are you concentrating?"

She wasn't. It was no use pretending that she was. There was still that nagging something—like a piece of dust in the eye or a shred of apple in a tooth. You could feel that it was there, but you couldn't get to grips with it.

There was a meeting at four o'clock, to decide whether they wanted to take part in a local drama festival, and if so, what were they going to do? Maggie attended reluctantly because Val had gone around telling everyone what a good organizer she was, but really her heart was not in it. Someone suggested Agatha Christie, and she couldn't even dredge up the energy to oppose it. What did it matter to her if they did Agatha Christie? What did it matter *what* they did?

A line had formed at the bus stop. She stood fretting and fuming, couldn't get on the first bus, got on the second, which deposited her at the foot of Station Road, ran panting all the way up the hill—and found Sunday sitting on her elbows on the gatepost.

"Sunday!" She swept her up. "Where have you been, you wicked, vile creature?" Wherever she had been, she was obviously very pleased with herself. Maggie held her out, shaking her. "You are a dreadful, dreadful cat!" The dreadful cat purred her agreement. Maggie didn't know whether to laugh or cry. All she could think of was: *Sebastian will be so pleased. . . .*

Together they ran up the stairs to his room, but it was only ten to five, he wouldn't be back from his parks and gardens for at least another twenty minutes. She went back down to her own room with Sunday, leaving the door ajar so that she could hear him when he came. She opened a can of cat meat, then, on impulse, leaving Sunday with her head stuck in the tin, scribbled a note— "CAT IS BACK!!"—and went galloping downstairs to stick it on the front door with a strip of tape.

She really needed to go over the road to the supermarket, she had only a lump of cheese and half a package of crackers in the cupboard, but she hung on as long as she could. She didn't want to run the risk of missing Sebastian; she wanted to see his face when he saw Sunday. At five to six, when he still wasn't back, she couldn't hang on any longer. The supermarket closed at six, and while the Indian shop on the corner was all right for popadums and curry powder, it was not much use for the ordinary staples of life, such as bread and butter.

At the foot of her note she added "GONE OVER THE ROAD." She half hoped he might come and find her there, but he didn't. He was obviously being kept late, though since it had been dark for the past forty minutes, it was difficult to imagine what they could be doing. Hardly hoeing the flower beds.

It wasn't until she sat down at seven o'clock, by herself, to eat a cheese and pickle sandwich, that she realized what it was that had been bothering her all day long. Slowly she stretched out a foot beneath the table; slowly she bent over to confirm what she already knew: Sebastian's boots. They were still there. Still standing there, on the newspaper, where she had put them last night.

Goose pimples broke out. The cheese and pickle sandwich turned to cardboard in her mouth. How could Sebastian have gone to work without his boots?

She forced herself to swallow. Her stomach, abruptly,

began pulsating; she could feel the blood banging in her head and the perspiration already prickling in the small of her back.

How could he go to work without his boots?

In all her life Maggie had never known fear. Not real, tearing, throat-drying fear. She knew it now, as she fled back up the stairs, with Sunday scudding beside her.

"God, don't let him have done it . . . please, God, don't let him have done it. . . ."

She didn't even believe in God. But whom else could you pray to?

She hammered so loudly at Sebastian's door that the Graces appeared on the floor below and Mick on the landing above. Mick hung over the banister. He was wearing what looked like a corset, but was in fact the latest thing in waistcoats from Odds & Sods.

"Hi, there, lady . . . what's with all the rough stuff?"

She tilted a distraught face toward him. "Have you seen Sebastian?"

"Not that I can recall. Why? Have you lost him?"

It sounded so silly.

"He's supposed to be at work, but—but he hasn't anything to wear, and it's dark, and—"

Mick grinned, broadly.

"In that case, with any luck, they won't catch him."

"C-catch him?"

"Streaking. In the dark."

"No, you don't understand! It's his boots! He left them in my room, they've been there all night—"

"Aha! Have they indeed? And where, one asks oneself, has Sebastian been all night?"

Could he *never* be serious?

"Mick, it's not funny!" she said.

"No, it's not." Unexpectedly Anthony Grace chimed in from the floor below. (She had discovered his name was Anthony from seeing it on letters: Anthony I. Grace, Esq.) "Far be it from me to want to make trouble, but I had been meaning to speak to you. You may not be aware of the way that sound carries in these old houses. It has a habit of rising up between the floorboards. And what with our bedroom being directly above yours—well." He broke off with a gesture.

"What he means," said Sandy apologetically, "is that you probably didn't realize you were keeping us awake."

"Until a quarter past three in the morning. I know it was a quarter past three because I looked at my watch. I was going to come down there and then, but—well."

"We didn't want to be unpleasant. It's just that we do have jobs to go to."

"Quite. We both hold down responsible positions. It's not as if—"

Pause.

Not as if we're just bums. Not as if we just do laboring for the city.

"Well. I just thought I ought to mention it."

"It won't happen again," said Maggie.

The Graces disappeared. Mick pulled a face and made quacking motions with his fingers.

"Great pompous nit. So what's all this about boots?"

"I told you." She ran a hand through her hair. (Unconscious imitation of Sebastian?) "He's left them downstairs."

"Well, so he's got something else, hasn't he? Shoes?"

She shook her head. She could feel herself almost on the verge of tears. What with Sebastian not coming home and now the Graces having a go at her—

"He's only got an old pair of sneakers. The soles are worn right through. He wouldn't go to work in those."

"You want to bet? Go to work barefoot if the fit took him! I've known him do dafter things than that. I told you about the time he got up on the roof? Back at Trinity? Fifty-foot drop. Could have killed himself. So he goes to work with his toes hanging out. Nothing to get steamed up about."

No, perhaps she was being silly and overdramatic. He *could* have gone off in his sneakers. He could have woken up, realized he'd left his boots in her room, not liked to disturb her—

"But, Mick, it's seven o'clock!" she said.

"So he's a big boy . . . stay out till midnight if he likes. Hey, now—" Mick swung himself down the stairs, one hand on the banister rail, one pressed against the wall, his feet not touching the ground. He landed, athletically, beside her. "What's all the big production? I didn't think you were the possessive type!"

She managed a smile: a bit tremulous but still a smile. Of sorts.

"Fancy some grub? We've got a stew on the go up there. One of Paula's specials . . . come on!" He punched her companionably on the shoulder. "Come and get stuck in. You don't want to worry yourself about old Brains—chances are he's living it up in the pub with some of his mates. Roll home at midnight, stoned out of his mind. You just forget about him. Come and drown your sorrows in a basinful of nosh."

She tried, but it wasn't any use. Like Sebastian the previous night, she couldn't be convinced. Every few mouthfuls she kept thinking up fresh objections. Sebastian didn't have mates; he was a loner. And he wasn't the sort to go "living it up" in a pub. He only ever drank to be sociable, and then not vast quantities. In any case— what about Sunday?

"What about her?" said Mick.

"He was so worried about her—"

"Worried about that?" Mick jabbed, derisively, with his fork. Sunday, busy helping herself out of the stewpot without having been invited, slowly lifted her head and regarded him with an air of cross-eyed disdain.

"She didn't come in last night. He was scared she might have been run over. He wouldn't just go and sit in the pub. He'd come straight back here to look for her."

"Well, maybe he did," said Paula. "Maybe he got back earlier, and she wasn't here, so he went off again."

"That'll be it," said Mick. "Have some beer?"

"N-no, thank you." She didn't like beer. In any case she was still troubled about Sebastian. "If he got back earlier, he must have got back before I did."

Mick said: "Yes," and reached across her for a glass.

"But that would mean he must have been out looking for her for over two hours!"

"It's a nice night," said Paula. She removed Sunday's head from the stew. "He's probably gone over the marsh. You know how it fascinates him."

The marsh.

Maggie set down her fork.

"Mick—"

"Mm?"

"You don't think—"

"Don't think? Oh, now, come on! Don't say *you're* taken in by his antics? Just a load of eyewash!"

People who talk about it don't.

Nonetheless—

She stood up.

"Come with me?"

"Jumping Jehoshaphat!" said Mick.

He looked at Paula. Paula hunched a shoulder.

"The stew will keep. But it's pitch-black out there. I don't know what you expect to see."

"Don't expect to see anything," said Mick.

They didn't go very far. Sebastian obviously wasn't there. Not unless—but she wouldn't let herself think of that. That, as Mick said, was all eyewash. *People who talk about it—*

"I'll just try his door again." She said it almost shame-facedly. "Just to make sure." If Mick hadn't been with her, she would have tried bending down and peering through the keyhole. Not that you could really see anything through keyholes, but—

"He isn't in there," said Mick.

"No."

She let her hand fall to her side. Mick considered her for a moment.

"Still not convinced, are you? . . . All right. Let's set your mind at rest."

"What are you—"

"Going to take a look."

"But—"

"Out through the lav window—climb along the drain-pipe. Simple."

"Mick!" She caught at his arm. "Be careful—"

"I'll be careful. Nothing to it."

Seconds later he was back again at her side.

"Okay, you can relax . . . not a body in sight. What were you expecting? Noose hanging from ceiling? Rivers

of blood? Great daft loon! He's obviously got you as
screwed up as he is."

"I'm sorry," said Maggie. She said it very humbly. She
wasn't normally the hysterical type. "I've gone and ruined your dinner, haven't I?"

"No need to apologize—one is, after all, a gentleman.
Any little service. What would you like me to do next?
Drag the marsh? Scour the railway line? . . . Lordy,
lordy!" He rolled his eyes. "Jus' my little joke, ma'am
. . . Tell you what! Why not try his folks?"

Maggie waited for a moment before replying. Then
she wiped her nose across the sleeve of her sweater and
said: "He d-doesn't g-get on with them."

"No? Well—no harm in trying. Never know your luck.
Might have had a brainstorm and decided to go and visit
'em. People do occasionally get attacks of remorse and
troll along to see their agèd P's. Even I—"

Yes, thought Maggie. But he probably didn't have a
father who called him a driveling idiot and said he ought
to be looked at.

"Go on!" said Mick. "Give it a go."

It was at least something to do. She had reached the
stage where doing anything at all was better than doing
nothing.

There weren't many Suttons in the book—she found
the number quite easily by running her finger down the
list until she came to one that lived at Farley Oaks. A
woman's voice answered. She said: "Muriel Sutton. May
I help you?" Very brisk and efficient. She might almost
have had the benefit of Miss Everton's tuition.

Maggie, with an agonized glance at Mick, because she
feared she was going to make a fool of herself, said: "I'm

sorry to bother you, but we're trying to find Sebastian. We wondered if—"

"Sebastian? My dear, Sebastian hasn't lived at home for—oh! It must be getting on for eighteen months."

"Yes, I—I did realize. We just wondered if—"

"He's got himself a room somewhere—somewhere in town. If you'd like to hold on a minute, I can let you have the address."

"No. That's all right." Maggie spoke rather desperately. This was obviously going to be a waste of time. "It wasn't the address that I—I mean, I have the address. It's where I'm ringing from. We just wondered if you'd s-seen him at all."

"Darling—" the woman called out to someone else. Her husband perhaps? "When did we last see Sebastian at all? Can you remember? . . . What? Really? Are you sure? Oh, well, if you say so. I hadn't realized it was so long. . . . Apparently the last time we saw him was back in the summer. Extraordinary how time flies!"

"Yes," said Maggie.

"Do I take it that he has—how shall I put it?—mislaid himself?"

"I'm sorry? I—I'm not quite sure I—"

"How long has he been missing?"

Maggie cast another agonized glance at Mick, who raised an eyebrow.

"We d-don't know for certain that he is m-missing exactly. It's just that he—he hasn't come home, and—"

"And you're worried about him? Yes, well, I shouldn't be if I were you. It's all quite usual. Just one of his little games."

Maggie frowned. The receiver, clamped in her hand, was hot and sticky. What was the woman talking about?

"When things get too much for him, it's just his way of coping. Last time it happened he was gone for almost four days. They finally found him wandering about the streets of Bishop's Stortford, of all unlikely places." Her voice became suddenly muffled; she must have placed a hand over the mouthpiece. Maggie could just make out the words "Seems he's gone and done another of his disappearing acts. His girl friend, I gather. Rather anxious." Then, back again to Maggie: "The next thing you know he'll probably have turned up in John o' Groat's or Land's End, claiming he has no idea how he got there. He really does choose the most extraordinary places! Did you by any chance—you won't mind my asking?—have a little disagreement or—"

Maggie changed the receiver over to her right hand and wiped the left one down the seat of her skirt.

"He was—worried—about his cat. She didn't come in last night—"

"Ah! Well—there you are, you see. That's your answer!" Again, the hand was placed over the mouthpiece: "Cat didn't come in. Obviously got in one of his states."

"The thing is," said Maggie, "she's back now, but we don't know where Sebastian is. We were scared in case—"

"Oh, my dear, I've told you! There isn't any need. He'll turn up when he's had enough. He never actually *does* anything."

What kind of woman was this? wondered Maggie. What kind of woman, who didn't care when her own son went missing?

"He was very upset," she said.

"Yes, he always is. It's all part and parcel of it. You mustn't let it distress you. Tell me . . . he was supposed to have been attending somewhere. Some clinic or other. Do I gather, from this, that he hasn't been doing so?"

Maggie swallowed.

"He's n-never mentioned it."

"In other words, he simply hasn't bothered." Mrs. Sutton made an impatient tutting noise down the line. Maggie heard the message being relayed to the unseen presence: "Hasn't been bothering with the clinic." Her tone implied: *Wouldn't you just know it?* Maggie felt resentment rising within her. So if Sebastian hadn't been bothering with the clinic—whatever "the clinic" might be—whose fault was that? Could it be his parents' for not caring enough to make sure? Maggie would have cared; she would have made sure. If only she had known.

In the background came the deeper rumbling of a man's voice. She heard Mrs. Sutton, in slightly querulous surprise: "Marcus, do you really think that's necessary?" More rumbling; then: "Are you still there, my dear? So sorry to have kept you. My husband was just suggesting —what is your name, by the way? . . . Maggie. And you're at the same address as Sebastian? Good. Just so we know how to get in touch with you should the need arise. My husband was suggesting that maybe—purely as a precaution, you understand—maybe we ought just to let them know. At the clinic. Not that we think anything is in the least likely to have happened, but one is never quite certain, when he has one of these fits. . . . How long exactly has he been gone?"

Maggie wiped beads of moisture from her upper lip.

"We're n-not absolutely p-positive. It's only that his b-boots are still here, and—"

"When was the last time you actually saw him?"

"About . . . three o'clock. Yesterday morning—*this*

morning." Her cheeks grew pink. "We were looking for the cat."

"So he could, in fact, have gone off then?"

"Well, he—he could. I suppose."

"Oh, he could, believe me! . . . Is he working or living off the state?"

This was like a nightmare.

"He's w-working."

"Where?"

"With the p-parks and g-gardens department." It had all gone out of control. Five minutes ago Sebastian had simply been late coming home: now, all of a sudden, he was missing.

"Parks and gardens. Right. Well, the police should be able to check whether he turned up or not. What was he wearing? Have you any idea?"

There wasn't much he could wear. Sebastian's wardrobe was hardly extensive.

"Probably j-just a sweater and j-jeans."

"Sweater and jeans. Dear me! Do you people never wear anything else?"

It seemed to be an attempt at humor. Maggie smiled weakly into the telephone.

"When it happened b-before—" she said.

"We were called all the way to Bishop's Stortford! Heaven only knows how he got there. We never did discover; he kept saying he couldn't remember. We must just hope this time he doesn't go so far afield . . . really, what a silly boy! How on earth does he imagine he's going to be able to cope with all the stresses and strains of being back at Cambridge if he won't even—"

"Back?" said Maggie. Mick, picking his fingernails on

the bottom step, paused to consider her. "He's g-going back there?"

"You sound surprised! Did he not tell you?"

"No. We thought—" They thought that he had been thrown out. It was what they had assumed—and Sebastian hadn't troubled himself to correct them.

"He only dropped out for a year—because of the Bishop's Stortford thing. They seemed to think he needed a sabbatical. Lots of good fresh air and no book learning . . . but of course, if he hasn't been doing what he was supposed to have been doing—" She broke off. Maggie could almost see the impatient hunching of the shoulder. Silk-clad by Jaeger. *"Such* a silly boy. He's got a brain— why doesn't he use it?"

Maggie didn't know whether she was expected to answer that one or not. She could have said that having a brain wasn't everything; one needed someone to *care.* But it might have sounded like rudeness, so she didn't. She just made a grunting sound, which could have meant anything.

"Anyway, my dear, it was sensible of you to ring—and whatever you do, don't worry. We'll get it sorted out. We'll be in touch the minute there's any news. And if by any chance he *should* happen to turn up of his own accord, you'll let us know?"

"Yes," said Maggie. "Of course."

She replaced the receiver. Mick said: "So what was all that about?"

"Sebastian's mother. She thinks he might have gone to Bishop's Stortford."

"Bishop's *Stort*ford?"

"Well, or John o' Groat's, or Land's End, or—or practically anywhere." She snatched up Sunday from the hall table. "It's all your fault," she said. She buried her face in the patchwork fur. "You stupid, *stupid* cat."

Sebastian did not turn up of his own accord. She left her note stuck to the door, just in case, and twice during the night she woke up because she thought that she heard him; but once it was Jimmy, falling up the front steps, and once it was a noise in the street outside, and although she flung open the window and leaned out and called, there wasn't any reply.

15

On Tuesday, during commerce, Maggie was called to the secretary's office, where she found a man in a shiny suit waiting to speak to her. The suit wasn't shiny because it was old but because it was made from some shimmering, slinky sort of material which had obviously cost the earth. The man inside it looked like a Hollywood version of Mr. Rochester out of *Jane Eyre*. Very tall, very dark, very imposing. Miss Johnston introduced him as Dr. Hegel. She didn't actually say that he was a psychiatrist, but Maggie supposed that he must be. She had never met one before. The parents always dismissed psychiatry as "crank stuff."

Miss Johnston said they could use Mr. Parker's study, since Mr. Parker was busy teaching commerce. She even offered to fetch coffee from the vending machine, but Dr. Hegel wisely said: "No, thank you." Most likely he had vending machines in his clinic.

"Then I'll leave you," said Miss Johnston.

She didn't ask Maggie if she would like a cup of coffee, which actually she rather would have, in spite of its being incontestably vile. Her throat had gone all dry again, just as it had last night, but obviously, as far as

Miss Johnston was concerned, a "no" from Dr. Hegel meant a "no" for both of them.

Dr. Hegel had come to ask her about Sebastian. He wanted to know how well Maggie knew him—the sorts of things they did together, the sorts of things they talked about. Whether Sebastian had ever confided in her.

"Ever told you anything about himself—about the way he might be feeling?"

He didn't have any sort of accent, even though he was called Dr. Hegel. He took notes, as Maggie talked, with a gold fountain pen. From upside down it looked suspiciously as if he were writing in shorthand.

Maggie told him all that she could. She told him everything except the bit about Sebastian's wanting to make love to her and her not letting him. And the bit about his feeling lonely and begging her not to go to sleep on him. They were personal. She didn't think Sebastian would want her telling things like that. After all, he had chosen not to go to Dr. Hegel, hadn't he?

"And there's nothing you can think of, no clue to where he might have gone if—let us say—he was feeling disturbed?"

Flinching somewhat at the phrase (it had awful overtones of "while the balance of his mind," etc., etc.), Maggie said that there was not.

"Nowhere he's ever mentioned? Nowhere that might mean something special to him?"

She shook her head.

"How about somewhere that you might have been to together? Somewhere where you've been particularly happy or had a particularly good time?"

She couldn't think of anywhere. She and Sebastian

had never really gone places together, apart from locally. They hadn't had the means. They had gone to Knole Park, of course, but that was where Sebastian had tortured himself with visions of vandals breaking in and getting at the deer, and she had yelled at him for going and ruining everything, and he had told her about his nightmares and about his father calling him a driveling idiot. He wasn't very likely to look back on Knole as a happy time.

She mentioned it to Dr. Hegel just in case, however, and he seemed interested and made a lot of notes with his gold fountain pen.

"So you went to Knole Park to see the deer, but when you got there, he had to go and ruin it all . . . just as he always did . . . visions of people maltreating the deer. You say he used to have nightmares about killing his rabbit and hurting the cat?"

Maggie frowned. She wasn't sure how much she ought to be divulging to Dr. Hegel. These were things that Sebastian had told her in confidence because he trusted her.

Dr. Hegel rolled his fountain pen between his hands. She noticed that they were beautifully manicured but that they had little tufts of hair growing on the backs of them.

"Miss Easter—Maggie." He stopped rolling the pen. "It is Maggie, isn't it? Yes, well, Maggie, we are both on the same side, you know. I'm only trying to help him."

"Yes."

"He does need help. You realize that, don't you?"

"Yes."

But if she could realize it, why couldn't his parents? They hadn't even tried. His mother hadn't even known how long it was since she'd last seen him. *Extraordinary how time flies.* . . .

"So. He had these nightmares. And used to torture himself with horrid visions—and then had to go and ruin everything by telling them to you." Dr. Hegel looked up at her. "How did you feel when he did that? Did it bother you?"

"Well—yes. Because it bothered him." There could be no harm in admitting that. "I didn't like seeing him so unhappy."

"But it didn't frighten you? You weren't scared that one day he might actually do something?"

She looked at him uncertainly.

"To the cat?" she said.

Almost imperceptibly Dr. Hegel lifted a shoulder.

"Sebastian wouldn't have hurt Sunday," said Maggie. "Sebastian wouldn't have hurt *any*one. He's gentle. He's a pacifist. He doesn't believe in violence."

"Then why, do you suppose"—Dr. Hegel leaned forward across the desk; he put the question very solemnly, as if Maggie were a fellow specialist with whom he were consulting—"why do you suppose he was so frightened of it in himself?"

"Because—" she floundered, seeking the right answer —"because *he* was scared he might do something to her."

"But why should he be?"

"I d-don't know."

"He's obviously very fond of her?"

"Yes." Apart from Maggie, Sunday was the only real friend that Sebastian had had.

"So if he's scared of hurting something he's fond of, we can reasonably assume that what he's really scared of is hurting himself?"

There was a silence.

"In other words," said Dr. Hegel, "it really is of vital importance that you tell me everything you can. *Everything.* Every place you've ever been to, every incident that's ever occurred, every remark he's ever made that's stuck in your memory . . . anything at all that might help us find him. Are we in agreement?"

Maggie nodded.

"Yes," she said.

Later that day Miss Everton gave them back their speed tests. Maggie's had a note at the bottom of it saying: "Did you really expect to get away with this? Kindly see me afterward." She honestly couldn't have cared less. How could she be expected to attach any importance to a speed test when Sebastian was missing? When he was lonely and unhappy and in need of help?

Miss Everton said: "Well, now, Miss Easter. And what have you got to say for yourself?"

Sometimes when people invited Maggie to say things for herself, she tended to overdo it and say more than she ought. Because when people said: "And what have you got to say for yourself?" what they really meant was "What excuse have you to make?" What they really wanted was for you to grovel and apologize.

It would probably have been easier to do just that; it would certainly have been more politic. After all, it wasn't Miss Everton's fault that Sebastian had gone off and that Maggie had done shorthand-typing only because of Val and that everyone had told her not to and that she wouldn't listen to them and that now she was bored out of her mind and Sebastian had said she would only be swelling the coffers of capitalism and she wasn't at all sure that she believed in it and—

Miss Everton, cutting without ceremony right across the middle of it, said icily that in that case she had better make an appointment to see the principal.

That was the second night that Sebastian didn't come home.

Next morning she saw Mr. Parker in his office. He was kind and paternal and told her that she was over-wrought.

"Because of this business with your boyfriend. I understand there are problems? Yes, well, it's bound to be upsetting. At your age—young persons take things so much to heart. All come out in the wash. Give it till the end of the term. See how you feel then."

Miss Everton said that if she was still going to be with them, then she had better do something about her short-hand. She said she could spend the evening transcribing the last three exercises from her *Pitman's Passages*.

"If you don't want to swell the coffers of capitalism, you can always go to Soviet Russia and take notes for the Kremlin."

Stupid woman. Stupid, *stupid* woman. She was stupider even than Sunday.

"But I want it done, Miss Easter. Understand that."

She would have done it; she had every intention. She took her books home with her. She even got as far as opening them. But it was at that point that the telephone rang, and it was Sebastian's mother, telling her that they had found Sebastian.

He had been wandering up the middle of the M1 motorway, among all the traffic.

"I just cannot think *how*—I mean, what on *earth* can he have been thinking of? To *do* such a thing? Such a silly, *silly* boy . . . he might have got himself *killed.*"

He hadn't even been wearing his sneakers.

16

"Poor old Brains!" If Mick had said it once during the past two days, he had said it a dozen times. The news about Sebastian seemed to have hit him really hard. He finished signing his name on the get well card they were sending from all of them and pushed it across the table to Paula. "I dunno . . . who'd have thought he'd go and do a thing like that?"

Maggie and Paula both looked at him. Maybe the same thought was going through Paula's head as through Maggie's: Anyone who had had eyes to see might have thought it. They all had chosen not to see; that was the trouble. They had preferred just to dismiss him as a pain. Sebastian is a drag, is a bore, is a pain. . . .

"It makes you feel like such a louse!" Mick catapulted his chair back from the table. Paula, in the act of signing her name, paused with an air of martyrdom. "The way we all used to lay into him—all those years at school. Taking the piss right and left. Everyone going around saying he's crazy. Saying he's bonkers. And then—"

Then it turns out that he really is? Maggie curled her fingers into the palm of her hand. Jesse, who had driven down from London especially to take her over to Dot's for the weekend, squeezed her arm reassuringly. Paula, meanwhile, was directing a succession of angry signals across the room to Mick. She had obviously drummed it into him beforehand: no orgies in front of Maggie. Sharply she said: "It's a bit late in the day for breast-beating."

"Yeah, I know. It's just that I feel like such a louse."

"So you said. You don't have to keep on about it."

"I'm not keeping on about it. I just feel like a louse. It's all right for you—you at least used to stick up for him occasionally. How do you think I feel?"

"You feel like a louse! But I don't see why you should expect to salve your conscience at everyone else's expense."

Mick collapsed gloomily onto Maggie's bed.

"What I don't understand," he said, "is how in heaven's name he came to be on a motorway in the first place?"

"I don't expect he does either," said Paula.

"And why choose the M1? That's what gets me."

Paula rolled her eyes. Birmingham, thought Maggie. It had to be Birmingham. It was the only explanation she could think of. Somewhere in his subconscious he must have been remembering Christmas. *Somewhere where you've been particularly happy together* . . . They had been happy at Christmas, just for a short while. Just for ten minutes, in the kitchen. And then they had been hauled back to reality, to a world where people said he was a pain and couldn't be bothered with him.

"He's got to have had something in mind." Mick, once started, did not give up that easily. "What makes a person suddenly go wandering off, in the middle of the night, without even any shoes on his feet?"

"That," said Paula, rather crisply, "is what one imagines they're trying to find out."

"Yeah, well, I mean, there's got to be some kind of explanation, hasn't there? People don't do things like that for no reason."

"No one ever suggested they did." Paula's tone was growing increasingly acerbic. Mick, like Chris, could be maddening when he chose. "That's why there are things like psychiatrists, right?"

"Oh, yeah . . . men in white coats asking tomfool questions. Fat lot of help they're likely to be."

Paula said witheringly: "You know nothing whatsoever about it. These people are trained. It's their job."

"To do what? Tell you you were raped in a hen run at the age of three and that's why you're terrified of chickens? Load of old rope!"

With sudden change of tactic Paula said: "I once read about this woman who had sixteen different personalities. *She* kept doing what Sebastian did—going off and not remembering. Only with her, she was someone different every time. Sixteen different people all in the same person. They got *her* better. You know what they did? They put her under hypnosis and took her right back to when she was still inside the womb. Made her remember things she didn't even know she'd known about." She turned, appealing, to Jesse. "They can, can't they? With hypnosis? They can discover all sorts of things."

Gravely Jesse inclined his head. "I believe in certain cases it can be quite useful."

"There you are then." Paula was triumphant. *"Not* just a load of old rope. They can actually get down to the root cause."

Maggie wondered why it was that sometimes when

people were doing their best to be positive, it only made you feel worse than you felt before. Maybe it was because Paula was trying so very hard.

"Listen." Jesse was looking at his watch. "I don't want to hurry you, but I did promise Dot that Maggie and I would be down in time for dinner, so—"

"Sure." Mick sprang to his feet. "Didn't mean to go on. Where's the card?" Paula handed it to him. "Do you want Them Upstairs to sign it, or just Jimmy and Peter?"

"Just Jimmy and Peter," said Maggie. The Graces were nonentities—and anyway, they had complained. "Don't forget to ask Jimmy for his Polaroid."

"No, okay." At the door Mick turned. "You don't think we—we ought to send him something more than just a card?"

"It won't be just a card. It'll be a photograph of Sunday." Saying the word "Sunday" had made her go all silly and weepish again. She had sworn she wouldn't do that. She groped for her handkerchief. "That'll mean more to him than anything." They'd never taken a photograph of Sunday. He would know, when he saw it, that she really was back, that it wasn't just something they were saying to try to make him feel better.

"Here." Jesse passed her his handkerchief, which was larger and more practical than hers. She accepted it gratefully.

Paula, embarrassed, said: "I'll go down with Mick. Back in a sec."

Maggie rubbed at her eyes. "Sorry."

"What for? A bit of emotion? Nothing to be ashamed of."

But it was, in the Easter family. Easters didn't cry. They looked life in the face; they were stoics.

"He was—s-supposed to be—g-going back to C-Cambridge in S-September."

"Well!" Jesse ruffled her hair. "September's a long way off. Another seven months to go."

"Do you really think that he'll b-be able to?"

"I should say there's a far better chance than there was before. At least now, perhaps, someone will be forced to sit up and pay attention and recognize the fact that he's not just posturing."

"Everyone always th-thought he was p-putting it on."

"All except you." Jesse winked. "Get yourself a gold star for that!"

It wasn't much comfort. What good had it done Sebastian? She was almost more at fault than anyone. The others, at any rate, had had the excuse of not realizing. Old Clever Clogs Easter, with her three A-levels, had realized. She'd known he wasn't just playacting—and what had she done about it? Nothing. Precisely nothing. Simply told him to go away and be neurotic elsewhere.

She screwed Jesse's handkerchief into a ball.

"Why didn't he tell us?" she said. "Why didn't he *tell* us he'd had to leave for a year? He let us all go on thinking he'd been thrown out. Why didn't he *say?*"

"Perhaps it wasn't very easy for him—it isn't, you know. Anything like that . . . people tend not to understand."

"But—" She was about to say, "He must have known that *I* would." And then she heard her own voice, yelling like a fishwife: *I'm sick of it! I'm sick of it! . . . Just because you don't care if everyone thinks you're balmy, it doesn't mean to say you have to make them think that I am!*

Why should he have told her, any more than the others?

"Maggie, sweetheart—" Jesse put an arm around her. He had almost never done that before. Like all the Easters, excepting only Dot, Jesse was undemonstrative. "You have nothing to reproach yourself with. You did more for him than anyone."

More, perhaps, but not half as much as she could have done.

Mick and Paula came back with Jimmy's Polaroid and the card, duly signed. Maggie had chosen the card herself. It had a big ginger cat sitting on the front, and inside she had written: "Dear Sebastian, Sunday is back!!! Fat and full of herself and not a *bit* repentant. Dot is going to look after her until you come home. Please hurry up and get well because I think she's missing you, and so am I. All our love, XXX Maggie and Sunday." Underneath that, the others had signed their names—Mick, Paula (with a wobble in the middle, where Mick had jogged her), Peter, Jimmy. Mick had added a cartoon drawing of a moon-faced man wearing a mortarboard, with a bubble coming out of his mouth which said: *"Digit extractum,* you vile boy!" He assured her that Sebastian would know what it meant.

They dug a protesting Sunday out of Maggie's eiderdown and sat her, blinking, on the table.

"Can we take more than one?" said Maggie. "He'd like that."

"Only on condition that you're holding her . . . he'd like that as well."

She was shy about being photographed because she knew she wasn't photogenic, but Mick insisted. He said she ought to be thinking of Sebastian, not of herself.

"After all, you mean just as much to him as that poxy cat."

"Compliments, compliments!" said Jesse. He jerked his head. "Go on, crone, have your picture took, or we'll never get over to Chislehurst."

They fastened Sunday into a collar and lead which Maggie had bought for her that morning and went downstairs to Jesse's car, Sunday trotting at Maggie's heels to the manner born, as if she were a dog.

"Isn't that fantastic?" said Maggie. "Isn't that really fantastic?"

Jesse said: "Yes, isn't it?" but he obviously said it only because it was expected. He didn't really think it was fantastic at all. He probably didn't realize how unusual it was for a totally untrained cat to walk about on the end of a lead. Sebastian would realize. She made a mental note that she must tell him. She had made so many mental notes of things that she must tell Sebastian that she was beginning to think she would have to buy a note pad and jot them all down.

"Can we just walk along to the box and post his card?"

"If we're quick," said Jesse.

She felt happier when she had seen the card and the photographs drop safely through the letterbox. A whole lot happier. She refused to believe that Sebastian could look upon a photograph of Sunday and not know who she was. He might not know Maggie, but he would know Sunday. She would get through to him. She would help him get better. Perhaps they might even let Maggie take her in to see him. That would be the best therapy of all. Why, by this time next week he could even be back in Station Road! Maggie would be responsible for him. She would make sure he did everything he was supposed to do. Go for treatment or whatever. After all, she couldn't be worse than those ghastly parents. They hadn't even tried. The doctors couldn't let him go back to them. And anyway, they wouldn't want him. That had probably been the trouble all along. It must be very dreadful not to be wanted. Perhaps they had never wanted him, right from the time he was born, and deep down inside himself he knew it, and that was why he— well, anyway, now that Dr. Hegel had charge of him, he could put him under hypnosis and take him back to the womb and it would all be discovered and then he could come to terms with it and it wouldn't make him un- happy anymore. Except—

Except that then he would know it on the surface as well as deep down, and for the life of her she couldn't see how that was supposed to solve anything. But maybe that wasn't the problem. Maybe the problem was some- thing quite different that only the experts could find out about. Just so long as they *could* find out. And if they could—well, if they could, they could do something. Couldn't they? They must be able to. You couldn't let a person go around being unhappy. Not as unhappy as Sebastian sometimes was. There had to be *some*thing. People like Mick, they were just cynics, they—

"Watch it!" Jesse put a hand beneath her elbow, steer- ing her to safety around a lamppost. "Daydreaming?"

Not daydreaming. She was an Easter; Easters didn't daydream. They faced up to life.

"Jess—" They were back at the car. Jesse was taking out his car keys, fitting them into the lock. He glanced across at her.

"Mm?"

"Jess . . . *you* don't think it's a load of old rope, do you?"

"Load of old rope?"

"Psychiatry—*you* don't think it's crank stuff?"

He smiled slightly. "You don't have to tar me with the same intolerant brush as the parents!"

"But you do think it's worthwhile? You do think it can help people? Like—like Sebastian?"

"If it can't, then the state's wasting an awful lot of money on it. . . . Oh, Maggie, of course I think it's worthwhile! And certainly it can help. No one but a fool would dispute that. Only"—he stretched out a hand across the car—"don't go expecting any miracles, hm? No sudden, overnight magic—"

"Oh, I know it's not like whipping out an appendix. I know it's more complicated than that. I just wanted to— to make sure."

Jesse unlocked the car; Maggie climbed in beside him. Sunday, with an air of consequence, instantly placed both front paws on the dashboard. Self-important, tail swishing, she surveyed the world from this new vantage point. (Something else she must remember to tell Sebastian: "Honestly, you'd think she'd been riding in cars all her life. Stood up at the window as proud as Punch . . .")

For a while they drove in silence; then Jesse, as if feeling the need to dispel any doubts he might possibly have created, said: "Of course, drugs play a large part in it these days. It's amazing what they can do with a few bottles of pills. Some of the latest stuff to come on the market—"

She listened with half an ear. Not that she wasn't interested, but—

"Jesse," she said, "how long does it take to become a psychiatrist?"

"How long does it *take?*"

Just let him dare to laugh.

He didn't.

"I'm not really sure," he said, "but a good long time, I
can tell you that much."

She frowned, pulling at Sunday's fur.

"How long would a good long time be?"

"Well, like . . . eight years, maybe?"

Eight years! Eight years would make her twenty-six—
and that was assuming she got started straight away.

"I suppose"—she fiddled nonchalantly with the clasp
on Sunday's lead—"I suppose one has to do a full medical training first of all?"

"Oh, yes," said Jesse.

"Yes. And I suppose—would you think—that one has
. . . left it a bit too late?"

Now let him laugh.

He didn't.

"I wouldn't think, at the age of eighteen," said Jesse,
"that one could have left anything a bit too late. Unless,
of course, one was planning to be a prodigy."

"Oh, well, yes. Of course. A prodigy."

"But if one merely wanted to gain admittance to the
portals of learning . . . the parents, I know, would be
delighted."

Yes, wouldn't they just? Wouldn't they crow?
Wouldn't they have a field day with the "I told you
so's"?

"We told you you were making a mistake. We said so
all along. We said you'd be bored within a week. We
said—"

Oh, well. Perhaps it was a small enough price to pay. If
it hadn't been for Sebastian, she might have gone off to

America with Val, and then it really would have been too late.

"Mind you, psychiatry . . ." said Jesse. "That's a pretty ambitious sort of goal to aim for."

Aim high; wasn't that what Pa always said? No harm in trying.

She made a mental note to tell Sebastian. At least he wouldn't be able to accuse her of swelling those dreaded capitalist coffers he was forever on about. That was something.

ABOUT THE AUTHOR

JEAN URE is the author of *See You Thursday*, a Junior Literary Guild selection and *What If They Saw Me Now?*, both available in Delacorte Press and Dell Laurel-Leaf editions. She lives in England.